a fortune foretold

A FORTUNE FORETOLD

a novel

Agneta Pleijel

TRANSLATED FROM THE SWEDISH BY
Marlaine Delargy

Other Press
New York

Production editor: Yvonne E. Cárdenas
Text designer: Julie Fry
This book was set in Whitman with Radiant and Britannic
by Alpha Design & Composition of Pittsfield, NH.

2 4 6 8 10 9 7 5 3 1

LIBRARY OF CONGRESS CATALOGING-IN-PUBLICATION DATA

Names: Pleijel, Agneta, 1940- author. | Delargy, Marlaine, translator.
Title: A fortune foretold: a novel / Agneta Pleijel ; translated from the Swedish by Marlaine Delargy.
Other titles: Spådomen. English
Description: New York : Other Press, 2017. | "Originally published in Swedish as Spådomen
by Norstedts, Stockholm, in 2015" — Verso title page.
Identifiers: LCCN 2016041050 (print) | LCCN 2016058185 (ebook) |
ISBN 9781590518304 (paperback) | ISBN 9781590518311 (E-book)
Subjects: LCSH: Pleijel, Agneta, 1940—Fiction. | Families—Fiction. | Marital conflict—
Fiction. | Self-realization—Fiction. | Lund (Sweden)—Fiction. | California—Fiction. |
BISAC: FICTION / Coming of Age. | FICTION / Biographical. | FICTION / Literary. |
GSAFD: Autobiographical fiction. | Bildungsromans.
Classification: LCC PT9876.26.L4 S6313 2017 (print) | LCC PT9876.26.L (ebook) |
DDC 839.73/74—dc23
LC record available at https://lccn.loc.gov/2016041050

Publisher's Note:
This is a work of fiction. Names, characters, places, and incidents either are the product of
the author's imagination or are used fictitiously, and any resemblance to actual persons,
living or dead, events, or locales is entirely coincidental.

I see that you live a selfless life. You care for an older person,
perhaps your mother, who is unwell.
There is something within you that I cannot fully interpret.
Perhaps it is in your mind, perhaps it is something outside you?
There are other things that I see clearly.
You will undertake a long journey, alone.
You will meet a dark man. He is in a relationship,
and you will have to endure a great sorrow.
If you do this, the man will seek you out.
You will be happy, and you will have two sons.
You will die in a white palace, by running water.

UNKNOWN FORTUNE-TELLER

IN THE LATE 1940S

1

landing and taking off

Being alone with an as yet unwritten book is like lingering within the first sleep of mankind.

●　●　●

Letters from family, letters from friends. I read them in the 1990s after the death of my father, and made a decent job of sorting them out. Life, the result of which is death, made no demands. And yet they complained a little. Whimpered. All those who are dead.

Not that they complain in the letters, but because their lives are over, and yet... unfinished. Once they were pressed close together, just as when the topmost branches of tall trees brush against one another, unseen by those down below, just as they do here by the old house in the archipelago.

I listen as I take the towels off the line in the mornings. The sound is melancholy. Helpless, somehow. It is August 10, and my father would have been one hundred years old today if he had lived. I sit in the room that was my Aunt Ricki's when she was a girl; it is very small, with a view over the steep drop down to the Sound. The trees have grown sky-high since I was a child. Down by the quayside there is a twisted pine tree.

It is old and in the process of dying, yet it still extends a gnarled arm out across the surface of the water. A child could lie there and read, like a character in an English children's book with lots of mysteries.

Quiet. Not even a sailboat to be seen.

I would like to understand what happened. And in what order. From memory. All the unanswered questions. Who were we? What is love? Surely a little love must linger, if it once existed? Otherwise there is only death and indifference. Memory is a liar, of course. I swim out into the warm August water. The girl who once was me, a child, can be seen far away in the distance, as if through a pair of binoculars turned the wrong way round. The others are there too. Far away in the distance. Like photographs that have turned to stone. I remember a photograph of Ricki when she was sixteen. A slender, sinewy body.

She is sitting on a garden chair in her swimsuit, a towel wrapped around her head. She is gazing out across the water; the pine tree is still full of life and vigor. She seems to be thinking hard about something. She looks that way in a lot of photographs.

In most of them I have not yet been born. But when I was twenty I went to visit Ricki in the Southern District Hospital; from the bus stop I thought it looked like a palace. That was the last time I saw her. Before the visit I had arranged to stay the night in her apartment on Drottninghusgränd.

It was stuffy and oppressive in the summer heat. I remember opening the window and closing the curtains.

Dropping to my knees in front of the bookcase.

Bergson. Freud. Nietzsche. Schopenhauer. Spinoza. Ricki's books. No one else in the family read that kind of thing. I made up the bed where I was to sleep, Ricki's little boy's narrow bed, with his Donald Duck comics in neat piles beside it. I couldn't sleep. I tried to masturbate, as I recall.

My approach was enterprising. Systematic. I wasn't a virgin, but had I ever had an orgasm, the way the sensation is described in Ernest Hemingway's *For Whom the Bell Tolls*, for example, when the earth moves?

There were two equally strong conflicting urges. To hold back, to give in. To let go, to maintain control. It became unbearable, and I gave up. My main objection to masturbation was the loneliness; it was such a powerful reminder that I was alone. Life consisted of disparate elements that were supposed to fit together, be placed in order, be reconciled.

I drank a glass of water in the bathroom.

I knew nothing about the person whose eyes I met in the mirror. I wasn't even sure whether I liked her. Probably not. I understood nothing. I hadn't a clue. Most of all I wanted just three things: to be free, to write, to have an orgasm. And later, much later, perhaps to have a child.

The idea of a child was so far in the future that it seemed like an illusion. I was worried about my visit to the hospital. I am trying to remember Ricki, but I am the one who takes center stage. Or rather she does — the girl.

• • •

My Aunt Ricki was an architect. For a long time she was employed by HSB, the Tenants' Savings and Building Society. My first memory of her — when was that? It was during the war when my father's younger sister came to visit us in Lund. I remember she spoke with a Stockholm accent.

I thought she sounded so funny; I made her repeat the same sentence over and over again, and it made me laugh every single time. In one of the letters — but I'll come to that later — it says that my father took off his wedding ring in 1948, and from then on he merely tried to put up with his marriage. Is that true?

Probably. But it was already too late. They had three children. It is only four years from my first memory of Ricki to 1948.

We came back from America in the late fall. We celebrated Christmas at my paternal grandparents' home. I can see the professorial apartment that went with my grandfather's job, but it is diffuse, in semidarkness. On the dining table was a silver bell that was rung to summon the maid (she was long gone, but the bell was still there).

Strained conversation. No one taking any notice of the children.

Christmas presents are handed out in the room known as the library. Cigar smoke and the cloying smell of soap drifting in from a long corridor. Book-covered walls, leather furniture. Everything appears as in a black-and-white photograph. Only Ricki is in color; that is because of the amazing present she gave me. A shiny box emerges from the wrapping paper. A magician in a black cape, gloves, and a top hat can be seen on the red lid. Inside the box are mysterious objects: glass containers, wands and cubes, decks of cards, dice and strings, a silk scarf that can be made to vanish or grow longer. It is all so dazzlingly magical that she cannot breathe.

She practices her sleight of hand in the kitchen at home in Årsta. Everything in the new apartment is unfamiliar. The harsh light falls steeply from outside. But as time goes by she is able to turn a small piece of string into a necklace with dangling beads. Command the dice to land with the sixes uppermost. Make invisible writing suddenly appear on a blank sheet of paper.

It is so exciting, it gives her butterflies in her tummy. It gives her power.

And from then on Ricki, who chose this present especially for her and who knows something about the secrets of transformation, is surrounded by a magic all of her own.

The suburb is newly built. Her maternal grandparents managed to secure the apartment for the family while they were in America, otherwise they would have had nowhere to live when they came home. From the balcony on the seventh floor you look down on a bare rockface and a chilly pine tree. The

7

development is still a building site; it is quite desolate, with long distances between construction projects. She is eight years old.

Curled up on the kitchen sofa, she practices diligently to make the hidden script appear, with its magic message. Her mother wants to play the piano in peace. She is given the task of taking her younger sisters down in the elevator. It descends with ineffable slowness.

Outside they are surrounded — herself, Ninne, and Ia — by hostile children. Cold, staring eyes. No one says a word. A little boy with white-blond hair prowls around them and breaks the silence. *They stink of cat piss.* The children laugh and disperse. In a trice it is as if they have been swallowed up. The playground is empty. Sunlight filtering through the trees, the blind facades of the houses. They don't stay long at the swings. What has just happened makes them feel uncomfortable.

More than that: they are frightened. She and Ninne, who is six years old, have started school in Årsta. It's a very long walk. They stick close together, followed by grinning little boys who fling insults at them. They are wearing the wrong clothes: American coats and headscarves.

It is snowing. It snows all the time, the icy wind whipping the wet flakes into their faces.

The schoolyard is teeming with unknown children. Why didn't she keep quiet about America? She is regarded as cocky and stuck-up because she has lived there. Her red plastic schoolbag doesn't help; it too smells of arrogance. And the way she speaks; her accent is a mixture of Skåne and America. She begs her mother for an angora hat, just like the ones most of the other girls wear: knitted in fluffy yarn, covering metal ear flaps. Blue or pink, and highly desirable.

Her mother can't see the problem.

She and Ninne are both kitted out in a beret, a ridiculous piece of headgear that her mother just happens to like. *Gustav Vasa*, the children shriek in the schoolyard, referring to the picture of the king on crispbread packets. She would do anything to avoid going to school, but there is no escape. The magician is kind to her; he provides her with transport that picks her up at the kitchen window and deposits her behind her desk in the classroom.

She is whisked back home in the same way, which means she doesn't have to speak to anyone, thank goodness. But the journeys to and from school make her head spin. She travels over cliffs and lakes, with sudden detours over forests and streams. Is she arrogant? No. She is locked in fear.

It is the spring term of third grade, and it is the fourth time she has encountered a new crowd of classmates. She found out a long time ago what it is like to stand there exposed before the hostile eyes of strangers. The children in Årsta are the worst so far.

She spends her time in the schoolyard all alone. She clenches her fists deep in her pockets. She is very frightened. The memory is strong.

· · ·

In the spring she turns nine, and Ricki, who gave her the amazing magic box, comes to Årsta one evening to babysit. At bedtime Ricki puts on a pair of white silk pajamas. Silk! They are allowed to feel the fabric: it is as soft as a caress. She smells delicious, of perfume or expensive soap. No lipstick, no red fingernails.

Her face is a little heavy, almost masculine. She speaks slowly, drawling in her Stockholm accent through her big nose. Never anything unconsidered, teasing, knowing. Other adults chatter about things that are irrelevant; not Ricki.

She is surrounded by an infectious aura of calm.

She has brought with her a set of architectural drawings from her job, and when the two younger girls have fallen asleep in the nursery, she spreads them out on the kitchen table. Houses for tiny little people. Have you drawn all these? the girl asks. Ricki corrects her: she has drawn only the toilets. A pang of disappointment — toilets! — but she furnishes the sketches in her imagination, allocates herself a room of her own.

Ricki thinks it's okay not to go to sleep right away. It's okay to read for as long as you like. That's what Ricki is going to do; she settles down with her book on Mom's couch. Everything is quiet. There isn't a sound from the living room. After a while she notices that Ricki has turned off the light, so she too switches off the light above the kitchen sofa, which is her bed.

In the morning she finds Ricki at the kitchen table in those wonderful silk pajamas. In the cold light of day, drawing toilets seems pretty unimpressive.

Have you got a boyfriend, Ricki?

Her aunt is drinking coffee and turning the pages of the newspaper, *Dagens Nyheter*. She shakes her head without looking up. The girl is embarrassed. How could she ask such a question when she is no more than an insecure nine-year-old? Who doesn't even have any friends. Who spends her time in the schoolyard all alone. Kerstin, who lives on the first floor of the apartment block, is one of her classmates.

She doesn't know Kerstin. Tanja on the fifth floor is in the same class as Ninne; her parents are immigrants. Tanja's father forbids them from eating ham, and her mother isn't allowed to smoke. Before he gets home she stands by the kitchen window, wafting the smoke away with a tea towel. If Tanja's father catches her, he beats her with a leather strap, the one he normally uses to sharpen his cutthroat razor.

Sometimes he beats Tanja too. Tanja's mother told Mom in the laundry room. She doesn't know them. She doesn't know anyone. And she keeps on asking Ricki about things that are none of her business.

Surely there must be someone who wants to go out with you?

Ricki measures half a teaspoon of sugar and sprinkles it in her coffee cup. No more than half a teaspoon. She is careful about what she puts into her body. Not too much sugar or salt (which allegedly binds water and expands the cells, making you fat. That's what she said last night).

No, Ricki says, rustling the newspaper.

She could have silenced her niece with a reprimand, but Ricki doesn't do that. She treats her as an equal, which fills her with astonished gratitude, a feeling she cannot put into words. She manages to say that she expects Ricki will soon find a boyfriend. She can't wait much longer. She is thirty, which is really old. Doesn't she want children?

Ricki glances at her without saying a word, while the girl ends her tirade with a reproachful, supercilious exclamation mark. *I'll soon be giving up on you, Ricki!*

Her aunt reaches across the table and cuts a couple of pieces of bread. She unscrews the lid of the marmalade jar, which was so tight that no one has been able to open it until now. She handles the cheese wire so adeptly that the white slices are thin and even. She goes for a shower and emerges from the bathroom fully dressed, with the silk pajamas neatly folded over her arm.

The girl is ashamed of herself afterward. She thinks she has upset Ricki. She thinks she has been overfamiliar and hurtful, just so that she could show off and make herself feel important.

She is ashamed. For many years. The nine-year-old. Insecure, but with a big mouth. I think I know why she was teased at school in Årsta. Not because she was arrogant, but because she always tried to behave like an adult, which was intolerable.

I didn't know that Ricki had been to see a fortune-teller with her friend Lisa; they were hoping to change their lives. But I was intuitive, like many children. Shame scurries in wherever it can find a foothold.

• • •

Ricki and her friend Lisa are invited to dinner in Årsta. Lisa's husband, who calls himself an inventor, is also there. After they have eaten in the kitchen, both children and adults move to the living room to play A Cargo Ship Comes Sailing In.

A cargo ship comes sailing in, laden with apricots from Andalucía.

With buns from Borås. And cherries from China. The inventor, red in the face, rocks on his chair. He is so drunk that he can't even catch the handkerchief rolled into a ball.

Long after everyone else has left the letter *B* and moved on, the inventor is still stubbornly struggling.

Breasts, broads, from... B-b-breasts and broads f-f-from...

He can't tear himself away from the breasts and the broads, and after a while Ricki and Lisa manage to ease him out of the apartment and into the elevator. Later on she wants to know what was wrong with him. They don't want to tell her, and only then does she realize it's something embarrassing.

Eventually Dad explains that he might have had a little bit too much to drink.

Mom is more direct, and says that the so-called inventor is a drunk. She can work out for herself what he wanted. When she puts two and two together, she feels sorry for Lisa, whose husband sits there bellowing about women so that everyone can hear.

Lisa is a dentist; her office is on Kornhamnstorg. Shortly after this incident the girl develops a raging toothache. Dad calls Lisa, who kindly agrees to see her even though it's a Sunday. While Lisa is drilling the tooth, the inventor turns up. She realizes this only when Lisa removes the drill from her mouth. He is demanding money, and has no intention of leaving until he gets it.

There is a scene. In her peripheral vision she sees Lisa fetch her purse and open it. *Don't ever come here again.*

When the inventor has gone, Lisa remains resolutely silent.

Which means that she can't say anything about it either. It's not the first time she has noticed that adults keep quiet about things that are unpleasant. By doing so they also force children to lie and dissemble. The most taboo subject of all is anything relating to sex. The mouth and the vagina have something in common. They are both unprotected orifices leading right inside the body.

When she is home alone she studies the reproductive organs in *The Housewife's Home Doctor*, five wine-red volumes on the bottom shelf of the bookcase in Dad's bedroom.

The woman has a hole. So does she. Judging by the hints in the books, it seems as if the male organ is inserted in this hole. Does this mean that Dad stuck his wiener inside Mom? Never in a million years. It's unthinkable. The gray expanse of uncertainty grows wider.

She quickly replaces the book when she hears a key in the front door. How does she know that she is doing something shameful? She just does. It is part of the far-reaching sphere of silence.

He's good, Vilhelm Moberg, Mom says to Dad. She is talking about the book they have both just read. There have been articles about it in the newspapers: it is regarded as indecent. The novel has been discussed in Parliament, according to Dad. When they have finished with the book she reads it too, under the covers with her flashlight.

The Emigrants, by Vilhelm Moberg, is the best book she has ever read. The characters are so brilliantly depicted that they are unforgettable: Kristina, Karl-Oskar. Ulrika from Västergöhl, who was called a whore, and that disgusting man whose penis stuck straight up in the air when he was dead. It's astonishing.

They have talked about seed and eggs. Not a word about the rest of it. Not a word about *sticking the wiener in the hole*.

Dad discovers that she has read the book. She is sitting on the kitchen sofa, drawing. Dad is leaning on the refrigerator. He runs his hand through his hair, as he always does when he doesn't know what to say.

So, you've read it. What did you think of it?

It was good. (In an indifferent tone of voice.)

Nothing you thought was unpleasant, or didn't understand?

Nope (shrug). Like what?

A cunning response. Dad drops the subject, but she can tell from his expression how terrible it would be even to suggest that he could do something so disgusting with Mom. She has no desire to embarrass her father like that. Thanks to *The Emigrants*, however, she is forced to acknowledge that this is what happens.

Everything points in that direction.

Before she read the novel she had no idea how a baby comes out — through the navel or the hole in your bottom? Now she knows that the baby comes out at the front, out of the woman's hole that doesn't really have a name. Mom calls it the front bottom. And although it seems unbelievable — how can a baby get through that little hole — the knowledge is invaluable.

In time she will be able to use it to show off in front of her friends. Unfortunately she still doesn't have any.

She reads all the time. Anything she can get hold of, and it started when she was very young. During her first year at school — that was in Lund, she started twelve months earlier than she should have done, because she had taught herself to read — she gets sick.

Scarlet fever with glandular complications, apparently. She is confined to an isolation unit at the hospital. No one is allowed in to see her, apart from the nursing staff who come and stick sharp needles in her bottom.

Penicillin is a new miracle drug; she has an injection every three hours around the clock, which probably saves her life. However, her buttocks are covered in scabs. She keeps on picking at them and crying.

Leaking like a sieve. Like a sponge that is being squeezed hard.

She waves to Mom and Dad through a pane of glass. They are both wearing thick coats and heavy boots; it is snowing outside. On one occasion Dad presses a handwritten note against the window. She reads it. There is a little boy in the isolation unit; he is sick too, and she can meet him if she likes. What a terrible idea! A strange boy!

No, no! She shakes her head so fervently that the meeting never takes place. She is very shy. Strange children frighten her more than anything. She sobs in her hospital bed, stubbornly and constantly. Until a tall, stern nurse in a black dress and a white hat — her name is Sister Ingrid — looms over her. *You do want to get better, don't you? In that case you need to stop crying.*

Because she is an obedient child, she stops at once. The nights are horrendous. She is afraid of the dark, and her tears keep her company. The only thing Mom and Dad can do is to send her books. One library book a day, and as long as that book lasts, she is able to stop thinking about them and missing them. She remains in the isolation unit for many weeks. Months, perhaps. She turns seven. Reading consumes her.

When she is allowed home at long last, her legs are so shaky that she can barely walk. She finds it difficult to grasp that the family has been there all the time, just the same as always, without realizing how *dreadfully* she has suffered.

Her stay in the hospital has made it very clear that they are perfectly fine without her. Don't they want her? A child that for some reason has deemed itself a failure becomes ingratiating. Like me. She is told that they are going to move.

Dad has been awarded a grant, and is going to carry out research at the Institute for Advanced Study at Princeton. It is mentioned frequently, which is why she remembers the name. All everyone talks about is America. No one asks how things have been for her.

•   •   •

They cross the Atlantic aboard the SS *Gripsholm*. Second grade in an American school and new classmates; this time she doesn't even have a language in which she can talk to them. She reads. Without her noticing how it happens, soon she is also reading American books. *The Bobbsey Twins*, about a family with several sets of twins. *Pollyanna*, who teaches the reader to be happy all the time. And *Alice in Wonderland* — unforgettable. Just like *Through the Looking Glass*, which is also about Alice and equally unforgettable. A step through a mirror, and anything can happen. She reads with such absorption that she forgets where she is.

In the spring they drive from Princeton to Los Angeles in a used car, a Nash, because Dad has gotten a job there. The journey takes ten days, and she spends all her time in the car reading.

At the drive-in, where they stop for hamburgers and Coca-Cola. At the motel. At the gas stations while the Nash is being filled up. She reads her way through the towns, across the prairies, along the sunlit Route 66. She reads through the Rocky Mountains and across the border into California. She puts down her book or her Roy Rogers comic — he is her hero among the cowboys — only when they visit an Indian reservation or stop to admire the Grand Canyon.

When they reach the Great Salt Lake Desert they travel at night, because of the heat. She lies on the backseat, Ninne on the floor between the front and back seats, and Ia with her head on Mom's lap and her legs on Dad's. The headlights illuminate the skeletons of animals and people. If they break down, death will be waiting for them.

According to Mom. Dad has wound down the window; he is smoking and resting his arm on the sill. The air is warm, wrapping itself around them. It is a memory that holds a sense of total security. A black sky arches above them. Unknown dangers lurk outside the car, but she is as safe and sound as a pea in a pod. Nothing bad can happen to her.

Not in this vast desert night. Never.

This is how she wants it to be.

Just the five of them. No one else.

She reads so as to hide where no one can get at her. That is necessary in Årsta. Mom is frequently in a bad mood; she has to shop, take care of the laundry, darn socks, vacuum the apartment, and put food on the table. She hates cooking, so it's usually Falun sausage and blood pudding. Nothing wrong with that; it's delicious.

Of course Mom sometimes plays her grand piano.

Mom throws her head back, her tongue moves inside her cheek keeping time with the music, her large hands taking charge of the keyboard, the magnificent sound filling the small apartment. A shutter comes down inside the girl's ear. It is because she perceives her mother's restlessness, her discontent.

But sometimes Mom wants to sing with them. She plays children's songs just as she did in Lund, when she was a piano teacher. She lifts Ia onto her knee and plays a Christmas carol.

You're musical, Mom says to Ninne.

Ia is too little for Mom to be able to assess her talent. But to the girl Mom says crossly: Keep your vocal chords together, don't let out the air the way you're doing now.

How do you keep your vocal chords together?

Where are they?

She loses the desire to sing. No, she doesn't want to. She sulks. Mom says she is *obstinate*. She looks up the word: stubborn, inflexible, self-willed. Is she all of those things? She understands that Mom thinks she has no musical ability; Mom ought to know, after all. She can't bear being criticized by Mom.

It makes her feel crushed. Unloved. As if the surface of her skin has been scratched to pieces. She loves her mom. She loves her very much, but she is afraid of her. Mom can easily fly into a temper. When that happens, Ia crawls under the piano and Ninne sidles off into the nursery. She herself tries to answer back.

You're not being fair, Mom. You're dumb!

But you have to be careful when Mom is in that mood. She just gets even more annoyed if you contradict her, and the girl turns into a frightened rabbit, wriggling to get away. Her heart pounds and she finds it difficult to breathe.

And the next minute, when Mom sighs and says that her life is passing so fast, she is compressed by guilt as if it were a clothespin. That's the worst thing of all, when Mom is unhappy with herself. When that happens the girl dangles there held fast by guilt, as if she were pinned to a clothesline. A guilty conscience.

She doesn't know where the conscience is either.

But it is gray and sludgy and it hurts.

We cannot see ourselves from the outside. But she stands at the window on the seventh floor and sees her mother emerge from the minimarket, its name, SNABBKÖP, written in red neon letters.

Mom is carrying heavy bags. She limps, because she had polio when she was young. Mom was seventeen years old; she prayed to God to spare her hands, and her prayers were answered. She could still play the piano, but one leg withered away until it was as thin as a twig, and that made her lame.

Poor Mom, limping through the park with her bags while Ia skips on ahead in the snow! She ought to run downstairs and help Mom, but there is a stone in her chest that stops her from doing so. A heavy stone.

It is made of granite, with a shimmering seam of quartz. The white quartz means helping Mom, but the granite weighs more. Mom and Ia make their way through the park as the streetlamps are lit. They need to cross the street, and Mom can't hold Ia's hand and carry the bags at the same time. She ought to go down in the elevator.

She doesn't do it. She just thinks about herself.

That's what Mom says, and she's probably right. She doesn't move until she hears the sound of the elevator; then she reluctantly goes into the hallway to open the front door for them.

•   •   •

Mom. Being with her is dizzying. Shininess and glitter and running water. With Mom there is satisfaction and relief. That's the way it was.

Mom takes her to see a lady who runs a children's theater company.

She has to read out a poem. It is a long, complicated poem by Erik Axel Karlfeldt, called *The Unrecognized Fiddler*. Mom has practiced with her at home. She is the scruffy fiddler; she reads with such insight that tears spring to her eyes.

If Elsa Olenius finds the ten-year-old a little comical — and she probably should have — she doesn't say so. The girl is allowed to join Our Theater.

Thanks to Mom. And all at once, everything can change. Mom becomes a dark forest, a volcano. When that happens, the ground shifts beneath the girl's feet.

She wants to be like Ricki, cool and unmoved.

Ricki comes to visit; she wants to give them her Tarzan books, three well-worn volumes that she found in the loft. She is giving them away because she is moving. Dad is at work as usual, even though it's a Sunday. Mom serves coffee in the living room, where the piano takes up most of the space. She seems annoyed with Ricki, her tone is impatient, why?

Mom once snapped that Dad's sisters are *insipid*.

Insipid.

No temperament, that's what Mom means. Mom, on the other hand, has plenty of temperament. She and Ricki are very different. In Årsta she has become aware of differences. At school there are children who smell of poverty. It is a rancid, acrid smell; poor hygiene, Dad says.

She knows that she is in a better position than others. She doesn't want anyone to find out that they have a grand piano. She doesn't want to deviate from the norm, and the piano is a clear deviation. The difference between Mom and Ricki hurts a great deal.

Ricki is sitting in the armchair, wearing high-heeled sandals.

Mom can't wear high heels because of her bad leg; she would turn her ankle. Ricki asks if Mom plays a lot. *And when do you imagine I would have time to do that? My musical life is over*, Mom replies. Her irritation is palpable, but Ricki doesn't seem to notice. She has made the effort to come all the way out to Årsta with the Tarzan books; there is no other reason for her visit. The girl is terrified that Mom will take out her discontent on Ricki. That Mom will complain about her life, her children, about Dad.

She likes Ricki; does that make her insipid too?

It is a conflict of loyalties. She has to get out of the situation. She asks if she can try on Ricki's shoes. Ricki obligingly kicks them off. They are too big, she totters along holding her arms out to the sides to help her balance on the high heels, and everyone laughs at her.

Neta is a theatrical little monkey, Mom says, stubbing out her cigarette. No problem. She is happy to play the monkey. They can laugh at her as much as they like. She has averted a dreadful threat. During Ricki's visit she has laid herself like a bridge across the river of differences. She has succeeded. There must be no differences.

And everyone must love one another.

If they don't, she will be split right down the middle.

Dad works at the technical college, and when he gets home late in the evenings, he tries to be helpful — washing up, vacuuming, cheering everyone up and telling bedtime stories.

It doesn't make any difference. Mom is still miserable.

Does he think Mom is *wasteful*? It seems that way. Mom is totting up till receipts. She is bent over the kitchen table, adding and adding, forgetting the cigarette in the ashtray. Then she shows Dad how much she has saved. Can't we move to a slightly bigger apartment? she begs. Dad doesn't answer right away.

We can't afford it, he says eventually.

I'm sure we can, Mom persists. I'd love to live in Östermalm.

Hmm, Dad says, and changes the subject.

He tells us a joke about a foolish student; Mom doesn't even smile. She is hurting inside. Dad washes the dishes. The girl dries. When the sisters have settled down in the nursery for the night, Dad lies down on Ia's bed and tells a story.

Never out of a book. He makes it all up. The story is about ants. Human beings invented the decimal system, because they have ten fingers. Ants have six legs. Their chief mathematician invents the seximal system and constructs a kind of catapult. They must defend their queen, who does nothing but lie around laying eggs; her name is fru Sextant. Dad laughs at his own wit.

The ants set to work with their catapult, bombarding the neighboring anthill with lingonberries and ants' eggs. She feels anxious as she listens. She doesn't understand why. Perhaps because Mom has closed the door behind her.

She goes back to the kitchen sofa and her book.

Sometimes Dad takes them with him to college so that Mom can play the piano in peace. Ninne and Ia scribble on the blackboard, while she reads the third Tarzan book and Dad loses himself in his papers, as usual.

Not long ago a moose managed to get into the college.

It was in the newspaper. It was seen running along the road somewhere near Johanneshov. During the night it came into town and got into the technical college. When it couldn't find its way out, it threw itself through a pane of glass. It was covered in wounds from the shards of glass when it was tracked down and shot.

On the bus home, Dad talks about the moose.

Maybe the moose wanted to be an engineer, Ninne suggests. Dad laughs and makes up a long story about the moose who wanted to be an engineer; the tale lasts for several evenings. The bus passes Enskede high school, where the moose started its education.

They applied for a place at Enskede, but her grades weren't good enough.

She didn't get a place anywhere else either, but she doesn't care. She and Ninne have been inside the gym at Enskede high school. Thanks to Mom, they attended ballet lessons there. A sour smell of sweat. Lots of girls, all in tulle skirts. Five positions with the feet, and *plié*!

• • •

One evening Mom takes her to a concert. They sit in what Mom refers to as *the gods*. The seats are so high up she feels dizzy. She can hear the murmur of voices from the audience far below; the people are so small they look like dolls. She can't even see the musicians.

This is where Mom used to sit with her friends from the Academy of Music. She talks about them. About Jussi Björling, the singer, who walked her home after a visit to the cinema and kissed her. About Dag Wirén, the composer; Mom was in love with him. The only thing wrong with him was the ridiculous belt on his coat.

The musicians are squeaking away down there; it sounds dreadful. She remembers Mom's comment about Dad's mom, who once said, *They scrape and scrape away with their bows, but do they get anywhere?* She is probably as unmusical as her grandmother. When she listens to serious music, that shutter deep inside her ear comes down.

At long last the concert begins. Mom closes her eyes and revels in the experience. The girl is bored to death. Afterward they plod through the darkness to catch the number 4. The blue streetcar passes the Royal Palace. She would like one of the princesses to get on, preferably Princess Désirée, who is older than her. Princess Christina would be okay too. If a princess sat down and started chatting to her, she would end up in a fairy tale. Princesses don't really travel by streetcar. So it's not going to happen. After the palace comes the Stomatol sign, with neon toothpaste squirting onto the toothbrush. It's fantastic! The whole city is covered in gooey toothpaste. At the last moment the sign goes off, unfortunately. They change to the bus, then they hobble home along Årstavägen.

She ought to be happy. She has her hand tucked under Mom's arm, and Mom is leaning heavily on her for support. Beneath the snow the ice is treacherous. *Change to the left foot.* She changes. Mom hates Årsta and the isolation. She wants to go to concerts, to the theater. Dad isn't really interested; he often drops off to sleep at concerts.

This evening as they limp home from the concert, she and Mom, making sure she uses the correct leg to keep in time, she feels the self-loathing sloshing around inside her. The concert tried her patience, but she ought to be happy.

Mom took her along, not Ninne.

Over and over again she decides to be happy. I'm really, really happy! Like Pollyanna. It doesn't work, so she has invented the paper doll. You can dress and undress a paper doll as you wish. She pretends that she is a paper doll. Mom wants to know if she enjoyed the concert.

The paper doll replies, *Oh yes!* Mom squeezes her arm affectionately and talks about the freedom in the music. Apparently it contains all the emotions for which there is no room in reality. She finds it difficult to understand what Mom means, but she nods anyway.

They turn off Årstavägen and walk under the dark arch leading to the supermarket. The snow is deeper here, and by the statue of the naked woman in the park Mom stumbles and falls. The girl is so terrified that her heart stops.

She manages to help Mom to her feet. Together they brush the snow off her coat. Mom swears; she is furious. Not because she fell; she is cursing her own uselessness. *You shouldn't get ideas above your station.*

The stars glimmer high in the sky; the light looks as if it is shimmering through thousands of tiny pinholes. They are small and cold, and yet it shines more brightly than the lights in the windows of the apartment block. It is absolutely freezing. *I'm an old cripple,* Mom goes on. *Good for nothing.*

They still have the long, icy hill on Siljansvägen ahead of them. That's not true, the paper doll replies, you'll be fine. Come on. They keep on limping. *I'm not even any use as a mother.* You're the best mom in the whole wide world, the paper doll exclaims with conviction. The distance between them is just as great as the distance to the stars. How are they going to get up the hill? The paper doll is determined to do it.

It is not possible to be entirely truthful.

You can't transfer what is on the inside to what shows on the outside. When they get home, Dad has fried Falun sausage and saved them some. The chunks of sausage look lonely, sitting there in grayish-white grease. Everyone is like that, she thinks. Each one of us is alone in a pool of congealing fat.

My mother was in a "convalescent home." For several weeks, presumably. I can't claim to recall the circumstances. The memory flickers past like a wisp of gray smoke. It was something that was never talked about, but my mother was definitely in something called a convalescent home with her mom and dad. They took her there because of her severe depression. Wasn't the home in Rimbo?

She turns eleven. She is now expected to look after her sisters when her parents aren't home. When they have gone to bed she sits on the floor in the study where her father sleeps and finds the section on the sex organs in *The Housewife's Home Doctor.*

Then she positions herself in front of the mirror in the living room.

Only the lamp above the green couch which serves as Mom's bed is lit. Her eyes in the mirror look feverish, gleaming like the eyes of a wild animal deep in the forest. Like the wolves in *The Children of Frostmo Mountain.* She pulls off her pajamas. A great deal has happened since the last time. Her nipples are no longer small and hard.

Something unknown is eating its way out of her body.

From the inside. That's actually how it feels.

She cups her hands over the breasts she doesn't yet have; she can sense a curve, something tender. She touches the bead of flesh between her legs. It brings a wave of heat, a shiver of fear, a stab of anticipation.

She lies down on the kitchen sofa and continues to explore the bead.

Recently she has touched it several times, usually very briefly before practicing her clown skills, such as bringing one leg up to the back of her neck from behind, forming the shape of a bow. But tonight she is obsessed.

Her belly is tingling as if she were on a roller-coaster at the Gröna Lund amusement park. She hasn't read about this feeling in any book. She is doing something you shouldn't do. She can't help it. She can't talk to anyone about this. Admittedly she has made some friends by now, like Marianne on Dellensvägen. She talks to Marianne about anything and everything. They found used rubbers on Årsta Field, and Marianne had an explanation at the ready. Some kind of fluid seeps out of guys, which means they have to wear a rubber over their wiener so their pants don't get wet.

They use a stick to pick up a rubber and examine it carefully.

But there is no way she can talk to Marianne about what she is doing now. She thinks she is the only person in the whole wide world who fiddles with herself like this. She knows she shouldn't do it. She knows she is doing something forbidden.

Nobody has told her, but she knows anyway.

The punishment comes the following summer.

They have borrowed her grandparents' summer cottage, and some of the children from next door have come over to play tag. During the game her belly starts aching. She bites her lip to help her cope with the pain.

When she pulls down her panties in the outside toilet, she discovers to her horror that they are stained with something brown. She sticks her finger inside her and it comes out brown too. Like shit. But it isn't coming out of the hole at the back; it is coming from the front. She examines the bead; thanks to the

Home Doctor, she knows it is called the clitoris. Is that where the brown stuff is coming from? So it seems.

She has contracted a serious illness. She has brought it upon herself. It's because she rubbed the bead; that's why she has to keep quiet about it. When the kids from next door have finally gone home, she clambers into the skiff by the jetty.

She takes off her panties and tries to wash away the stains. The skiff bobs up and down in the swell from the boats. She almost falls overboard when the steamboat from town passes by. The water is ice cold. The pain is agonizing.

She scrubs away in despair; the stains are still there.

What is she going to do? Row out to sea, heading toward Finland, and drown. By the time her skeleton is found, the fish will have eaten her panties and no one will be able to accuse her of anything. Will they miss her? She hopes so, and the thought sweetens her misery a little. It is absolutely impossible to get rid of the stains.

What on earth are you doing? Mom is standing on the jetty, wearing those horrible men's corduroy pants. There is no chance of hiding the terrible thing that has happened. Not a word about the fiddling, never. But she has to come clean about the stains.

Mom laughs, although she doesn't sound particularly happy, and tells her that it's *her time of the month*. What does that mean? Mom says it's menstruation, the curse, her period. Unusually early, she says, you're only eleven, but it probably runs in the family. According to Mom, girls mature more quickly in the tropics, where Granny comes from.

The fact that women bleed is nothing new.

She read about it in the *Home Doctor*. In *The Emigrants* some of them actually bleed to death. But is this brown stuff supposed to be blood? Mom digs out something crocheted and disgusting to wear between her legs. After dinner she is drying the dishes when Mom unexpectedly gives her half a bar of Marabou milk chocolate.

Because you've become a woman.

Has she? Mom sounds a little sarcastic. She can hear her sisters yelling upstairs. Outside, darkness is falling. Through the half-open door leading to the dining room she can see her father, absorbed in his papers as usual. He is sitting in a warm circle of light from the ceiling lamp, which has a fringe made of tiny glass beads.

He makes her feel safe; he is rarely as impatient as Mom. But at that moment, as she stands in the doorway and catches sight of her father, she is overwhelmed by a sense of shame that is worse than anything she has ever experienced: long, hot waves of shame. Please don't let him find out. But Mom is bound to tell him, of course.

They will laugh at her behind her back. She is alone and disgraced and more isolated than ever before, at the mercy of the authorities and abandonment.

Before this happens — before she is stricken with the horrors of menstruation — she learns that she has gotten a place at the high school in Hökarängen after all.

She actually receives the telegram while she is staying with her grandparents in the country; her mother sends it on from town. First of all it is read out to her over the wind-up telephone, then the postman turns up on his bicycle with the real thing. *Congratulations to our high school girl!* With a picture of a Swedish flag. Mom is obviously delighted. So is Granny. Another new school? She feels like the moose who got trapped and then shot. She doesn't want to start all over again.

She is standing on the pier waiting for the steamboat bringing her mother from town. Mom has to stop this happening, make sure she doesn't have to change schools.

The boat is still some distance away when she spots her beautiful mother, standing on the foredeck with her face turned up to the sun, wearing a red jacket that glows like a traffic light. She feels a physical pain in her chest; she has missed her mother so much. The longing is fierce, immeasurable.

Is that the way it was? Yes. That was before I began to menstruate. I dug out the memory of my longing on the steamboat pier much later, when I thought I had never yearned for my mother.

The strength of the emotion within the memory convinced me that wasn't the case. Feelings have an archaeology; you can dig down, discover new things.

And a child is an hourglass, measuring out the life of an adult. Mom had just turned forty, and was beginning to feel old. She was unprepared for the fact that I was growing so fast, and perhaps a little disturbed by it. We never talked about it. Never. Menstruation: I avoided the word for many, many years.

The next time it happens is in Årsta. Mom is sitting in the living room, darning socks. She glances up and her expression freezes slightly.

Aha, she says dryly, putting aside the darning mushroom. From her mother's tone of voice, she gathers that they are both equally embarrassed. Perhaps Mom had hoped that the ordeal wouldn't be repeated.

This time she is given a sanitary towel made of fabric. She has to wear a cotton belt around her waist, with two thin pieces hanging down that pass through the loops at either end of the towel, holding it in place. It's very complicated, and the belt keeps getting tangled up. She stands in the bathroom trying to sort it all out.

Outside in the hallway, Mom is getting stressed. There isn't much time; they're supposed to be going somewhere. The belt is still playing up, tying itself in knots. Mom gets more and more impatient; she hammers on the door and yells, *Haven't you got that goddamn towel on yet?*

Her sisters are waiting out there too, as curious as magpies.

She wants to die right there in the bathroom with that goddamn towel. There is no doubt that Mom is angry about her period, but she has to walk out and face everyone. She holds her head as high as she can. She refuses to answer Ninne's questions — what goddamn towel, what is Mommy talking about? — as they leave the apartment.

It turns out that some of her classmates from Årsta have been accepted at the same high school as her. One of them is Annemarie, who lives on Siljansvägen; she is to call for her in the mornings. It is still dark as she crosses the street.

She has to wait in the hallway for a long time, sweating in her winter clothes.

Annemarie is an only child, and her parents flutter around her like two anxious butterflies. She must put on a different scarf, change her socks for thicker ones, have Nivea smeared on her cheeks. Annemarie simply lets them carry on.

Meanwhile she waits under a picture of two horses. She hates Annemarie for all this messing around. No one fusses over her. She has to leave home before anyone else. Dad wakes her early with a cheese sandwich. The others are still sleeping, Mom with a pillow over her head.

She is envious of Annemarie, and she feels *evil*.

Yes. I was extremely envious.

I enjoyed feeling evil.

They plod along in the darkness, all the way up Årstavägen to the stop for the number 77. Annemarie is wearing a Lapp hat with a colorful tassel right on the top. Out of the corner of her eye she can see that ridiculous tassel bobbing around. They have nothing to talk about.

At Johanneshov they change to the new subway. They have gotten into Gubbängen high school, which at the moment is no more than a few classrooms along one corridor in Hökarängen junior school. The schoolyard is rough and noisy and the boys are fighting. During every recess a horde of yelling boys chases some long-legged girl. Their quarry is yelling too; maybe she likes being chased. The toilets are in the yard in a separate building. The cubicles have no doors. The boys hang around outside the windows of the girls' toilets, spying on them. She hates the toilets. She finds it difficult to cope with the sanitary towel, the white cotton belt, and the embarrassment. At the end of morning recess one day she bumps into the girl who always gets chased. She is stumbling up the steps from the cellar, zipping up her pants.

Her cheeks are bright red and wet. The boys must have dragged her down into the cellar. What have they done to her? She meets the girl's eyes, her expression is... flayed. That is the word the memory delivers. Skinned. *Flayed.* Next recess they are chasing her again.

However, she immediately likes the person sitting next to her in class. She is thirteen — a couple of years older. One of the reasons why she likes Barbro is that she too is having her *monthlies.* She doesn't know anyone else in the same position.

During recess Barbro tells her that she was sitting in class at junior school when the blood started pouring down her leg. It was like Niagara Falls, Barbro says, laughing.

Barbro stood up, wiped the chair with her skirt and went home. She finds Barbro uncompromising and courageous. She has large breasts and the boys shout *Big Boobs Babs* when she walks past, but Barbro doesn't give a damn. Her father is a cab driver. She travels with Barbro to Skanstull, where he waits in his cab. They are on their way to Åhlén & Holm, the department store, to look for small lipsticks for thirty-five öre.

Barbro taps on the window and holds out her hand.

Her father sighs, grins, and hands over some money. A close family, she thinks as she stands beside Barbro; once again that stab of envy.

She also goes home with Barbro after school. Her classmate lives in a recently built apartment in Hökarängen, several rooms, no furniture apart from six beds, rather whimsically distributed throughout the place. They sit on the kitchen floor in a strip of sunlight eating sandwiches, there are no chairs. Barbro has three older brothers. Between mouthfuls she confides that she got sick of everyone bossing her around, so one day she got into bed with a breadknife, pulled up the sheet, and splashed tomato ketchup all over it.

The perfect suicide.

She was determined to make her point. She waited. The others came home and her mother screamed like a stuck pig. Afterward they all laughed and agreed that it was a cool thing to do. What would have happened if the girl had done the same thing at home?

She admires Barbro for her courage and directness. She also likes Barbro's mother, whom she never gets to meet.

These are pictures from another life. Tangled up in emotions, still heavily charged. Most are blurred, but some stand out with great clarity. One morning Barbro arrives late. She slinks in during Swedish, slides into her seat.

Barbro quickly shows her the note her mother has sent in. It begins: *Engwall!!!* Three exclamation marks. It is immediately obvious that the note is full of spelling mistakes, and is badly written with clumsy, unfinished sentences and unnecessary exclamation marks.

But what has happened is conveyed very clearly. An alarm clock didn't ring, chaos, everyone overslept. Barbro wonders in a whisper whether the note will do? Absolutely. There is no possibility of misinterpreting the contents. The Swedish teacher — everyone is afraid of her and her pointer — reads the note and frowns. She picks up a piece of chalk and writes *Dear Miss Engwall* on the blackboard, then underlines the words three times. In front of the whole class she picks out the spelling mistakes Barbro's mother has made, corrects them, then gives Barbro a good telling off. *Lack of knowledge and education,* says Engwall, plus *lack of respect.*

She is to be addressed correctly: *Dear Miss Engwall* is the appropriate form in a written communication. Barbro is held responsible for every error in her mother's note. She sits there with her head down, cheeks bright red. It is so embarrassing. And unfair on Barbro.

Afterward they walk up the slope behind the school and sit down, leaning against the trunk of a pine tree. Barbro wants to hear more of the dirty bits from *The Emigrants.*

The spring sunshine is warm. There are patches of wood anemones growing among the trees. They are not best friends; Barbro has lots of other friends. But she likes Barbro, who listens and seems to know what it's all about.

· · ·

I know the subway stations off by heart. I also remember the images that went with them as I traveled beside a silent Annemarie.

Johanneshov (now Gullmarsplan): *silence, not a sound, the world is sleeping.*

Blåsut: *reveille, a trumpet, a knight on a horse.*

Sandsborg: *a sand castle, the sand trickling down, the roar of the sea.*

Skogskyrkogården: *music, trees, a stone wall, graves, sometimes it hurts so much, will I die too? Not for a long time. Life is long.*

Tallkrogen: *lots of pretty little houses with pretty little lights.*

Gubbängen — Old Man's Meadow (this one lasts all the way to the next station): *old men fumbling and stumbling, boozing and snoozing, belching and squelching, stuttering and muttering, creeping and sleeping, snoring and boring, huffing and puffing, wheezing and freezing, drinking and stinking, pissing and missing...*

Hökarängen: the last stop, and the rhyme comes to an abrupt end. Everyone is in a hurry, the clatter of heavy boots, pushing and shoving, lots of kids get off here and they shout and scream in the concrete stairwell, the racket is deafening.

Laila (who lives in one of the new apartment blocks for families with three or more children in Årsta, and who is achingly cool and cheeky): Have you heard? Tumba-Tarzan is at it again!

Birgitta (whose parents give her twenty-five öre for every book she reads, imagine that!): Tumba-Tarzan doesn't exist, he's just something the newspapers have made up.

Laila: He so does exist — you be careful, he could turn up at any minute!

The girl (slightly vague): Who's Tumba-Tarzan?

Laila (forcefully): Jeez, you know nothing — sometimes I wonder if you've even been born yet, he hangs out in the forest, he robs empty summer cottages, the cops can't catch him, my dad says...

But the girl is no longer listening. He is walking just a little way ahead of her, along with two guys in windcheaters carrying hockey sticks. He's wearing a red woolen hat. She takes in the slim neck. The narrow ass. Boys have slimmer bodies than girls; she is always trying to clench her buttocks. He has chapped skin and red hair, he is German, he lives in Årsta, and she is in love with him.

One day she will leave a note in his desk, telling him. An anonymous note, of course. Laila links arms with her, Birgitta does the same on the other side. They walk to school pressed close together.

Everything is better. No one teases her anymore, at least not so much that it bothers her.

I don't recall my parents ever visiting the school in Hökarängen. Dad probably came with me on my very first day. But I do remember other things.

She sold May flowers in the spring and Christmas magazines in the winter.

They organized a class party, even though Engwall said they weren't allowed. She and Marianne managed to get into the Forum cinema in Årsta to see *One Summer of Happiness*, even though it had an adults-only certificate and she was twelve and Marianne thirteen. She went out on her skis and the snow on Årsta Field was sparkling white with blue shadows.

And love. The red-haired boy is lying with her on the kitchen sofa. Well, not really, but he's very close. She can hear him breathing. They don't do anything in particular, they're just very close. The only thing that happens is that he sometimes cries like a girl — *why?* — and she comforts him.

To be honest, in reality that is, she doesn't exchange a single word with him, except on one occasion when they are caught up in the crush at the main door leaving school. He raises his arm and she pushes it down. He gives her a long look.

What the fuck!

That was probably the only time he noticed her.

She hides her feelings because they are so strong. To declare one's love is to be exposed, irredeemably lost. In spite of this, one day she sneaks a note bearing those three words into his desk. No signature. It is in the spring of second grade, and she has just found out that she will be leaving school, because they are moving again.

She slips the note into his desk before anyone else arrives in the classroom. From her place at the back she sees him open the lid, pick up the note, read those three words, glance suspiciously over his shoulder, then crumple up the scrap of paper. Well, at least I told him, she thinks.

She has never lived anywhere as long as in the apartment in Årsta. Three and a half years. And now they are moving again. She thinks she has made an enormous effort. Taken all kinds of crap. Put up with being teased. She hasn't complained — whom would she complain to? — and finally she has succeeded. She has made some friends. Have all her efforts been in vain?

There is a lump of sorrow sitting inside her. She herself is that disgusting lump. She rests her cheek on the window, all alone on the way home in the coach with the dirty yellow walls and the green plastic-coated seats. She always has to wait for the bus at Johanneshov.

There is a long line.

It is cold, a biting wind with snow in the air.

When the bus finally shows up it is already overfull. People swear and complain because they can't get on. The conductor yells at them from his ticket office, telling them to stop trying to push through. She has to wait for the next bus.

She is frozen and hungry. She cries inside. Far too often. The following morning she has to catch the bus again, traveling in the opposite direction this time. There is no point to anything, no point to her. She doesn't understand where this sorrow comes from, but it overwhelms her.

Yes, of course, they're going to move, and she doesn't want to.

But the sorrow is bigger than that. And it's *vicious*. Just as when some nasty kid squeezes together a hard ball of ice, takes aim, and hits you on the back of the neck so that you fall flat on your face. Out of the darkness comes a horrible laugh. Somewhere in a strange room that she can't see, unknown beings have weighed and considered and found her wanting.

• • •

During all those years in Årsta she has longed for a dog. A real dog, a Schnauzer. No chance. On the beach in Santa Monica in California they knew a married couple with two Schnauzers, one brown and one black.

The dogs leap out from the backseat of the car, barking joyously as they race toward the ocean. She runs alongside them. She swims with them. She hunts in the sand for the empty shells of giant turtles, the colors shimmering on the inside. She clambers up a great big sand dune, and deep inside a thicket of scratchy undergrowth she finds an old, rotting wooden sign. She moves her index finger over the semi-obliterated letters. With some difficulty she manages to work out what it says:

NO BLACKS. NO DOGS. NO JEWS.

There are plenty of dogs around, and some black people too. Who isn't allowed on the beach? She wants to know what *Jews* means. Mom has bought an elegant white swimsuit with a palm tree over one hip, and she is wearing black sunglasses.

Forget it, Mom says. It's just an old sign.

When she persists, Mom points to the pretty girl with long blond hair, sitting alone on a blanket letting the sand trickle through her fingers. She is Paco's girlfriend. Paco is a Swedish-American, and he is Dad's colleague. The two men are standing at the water's edge in swimming trunks conducting a discussion, as mathematicians always do. The young girl on the blanket has a number tattooed on her arm.

She has noticed it before. Mom says she is a Jewess, and has been in a concentration camp. She asks more questions, and learns what happened to the Jews during the war. She doesn't understand it, and wants to stop thinking about it.

But all it takes is the sign for Sandsborg outside the window of the subway train, and it all comes flooding back: the beach, the sand, the turtle shells, the Schnauzers, the wooden sign, and the girl sitting on a blanket all alone.

And the lack of love. She doesn't have room for all this.

Lack of love? A big concept. Far too big, perhaps.

But she tries to find a sausage skin so that she can stuff life inside it and tie up the end, so that it all fits together. She can't get life into the sausage skin.

She knows that she has a better life than most people. But there is a shortage of love — no more than the odd glimpse from time to time. It's not just because they are moving and she will never see the red-haired boy again. There's other stuff too. The old guy she and Annemarie tripped over on the way to the bus. He was dead.

A homeless old man, poor and covered in snow. A hobo, people said.

And Tanja's dad, who jumped out of a fifth-floor window. They took him away in an ambulance, but they couldn't save his life. Why did he have to jump out of the window and die? He was unhappy, of course. But *why*?

And then there's Mom and Dad, who have almost stopped speaking to each other. Dad tells stories, does the dishes, and tries to cheer everyone up, but it doesn't help. When he notices that none of this makes Mom feel any better, he becomes distant, as if a veil is drawn over his face. It's impossible to get a word out of him.

And then she gets scared. What's going on?

She keeps a careful eye on herself, like King of the Royal Mounted. She needs to blend in. Be good enough. Be accepted. Avoid irritating Mom. Stop being nasty to Ninne (she doesn't quite manage that one). She is kind to Ia; Ia is her baby.

But the shapeless fear — the thing that language cannot frame, however many new words she has learned — continues to threaten her. She goes out onto the balcony. She can see the roof of the block where the red-haired boy lives. She can see all the way to the sign on the NK department store, constantly rotating. On one side there are the green letters, NK, on the other the clock. She doesn't know anyone in Lund.

• • •

Outside their front door is a short staircase leading up to the balcony where the residents can go to beat their rugs. Opposite the balcony is a gray steel door, which is locked. And behind that door lives a strange creature: alone, confined, orphaned. Dirty and scruffy.

Barely even human. Resembling a starving animal. She collects food for her over the course of many nights. Leftovers from the refrigerator. A solitary boiled potato. A few dried-up slices of sausage. Crusts of bread. Anything at all. She takes the plate upstairs and bangs on the door.

The creature inside is very frightened. It takes a while, but eventually the door opens a fraction. And this female creature, crazed with hunger, trembles and gobbles everything so savagely and unselfconsciously that it is a strangely enjoyable spectacle. The creature would die if she didn't bring her the leftover food. She is kept alive only with the help of the worst, the most disgusting scraps. She needs so little, and is grateful for the smallest contribution.

She is company. She is there during the course of many long nights.

She is there for ages, all the time they are living in Årsta. When the girl feels unhappy, she gathers together the leftovers for the creature, which survives purely on what she can spare from her own excess, her incomparably richer bank of resources. The creature enables her to feel a little better than she actually is.

But one boring Sunday when she doesn't have anything to do, she calls Ricki and asks if she can come over and see her. She catches the bus to Ricki's new place on Banérgatan, and Ricki meets her at the stop with a bag of pastries in her hand. She is stylish in a white suit and high-heeled shoes. The apartment is small and dark, one room with a tiny kitchenette. It is sparse and bare. One bookshelf. A round coffee table, two chairs, and a bed. That's all. At home there is always stuff everywhere, magazines and papers, clothes lying around that make Mom curse, Ia's toys, potted plants crowding the windowsills. Ricki's apartment is pared to the bone; it looks like a storage depot.

Not a single picture on the walls. Nothing apart from a guitar, hanging up. It seems to be screaming *Touch me*, and it has several small droopy silk ribbons knotted around its neck. It's the only personal thing she can see, apart from two straw-covered empty bottles on the bookshelf.

Has Ricki tidied up for her, a child? Or does it always look this way?

Ricki pours them each a glass of juice in the kitchenette while she waits on one of the chairs. They drink their juice and eat Danish pastries and talk about Tarzan, Cheetah, and the language of the apes. Ricki has seen the film, and says that Johnny Weissmuller is handsome.

After a while they don't really have much to talk about.

Ricki doesn't ask her any questions. And what would she ask Ricki? There is nothing to suggest that Ricki has friends, a social circle, interests, or anything that might involve having fun—a life outside the sphere of HSB and its toilets, to put it briefly. She knows that Ricki doesn't have a boyfriend.

But she really likes Ricki. When she has finished her juice, she realizes she ought to make a move. She says she should be going; it all feels a little awkward. However, when they are on the way out, Ricki says with genuine warmth in her voice that she has appreciated the visit, and hopes she will come again.

Ricki walks her back to the bus stop and waits with her until the bus arrives. *Mysterious* is a good word for Ricki.

Dad buys a used Hanomag, it's a German car, and he gets it cheap. They will be traveling to Lund in the car; Dad has become a professor there. They have to say goodbye to everyone. Goodbye to her paternal grandparents, who have moved to a three-room apartment in Västertorp.

They have often cycled over there on Sundays. Mom wants to play the piano, so Dad goes down to the cellar to pump up the tires with a grim expression on his face. He slips on his cycle clips and settles Ia on the parcel shelf. Ninni cycles in the middle, wobbling along.

The girl brings up the rear. Sockenvägen is long and depressing, and the sun is beating down. An afternoon spent with her grandparents is indescribably boring; she just wants to die. But this time they have arrived by car. Mom isn't with them.

Ricki is in the kitchen, making sandwiches! Her soft hair is caught up in a clip at the back of her neck, and she looks a bit like the model and film star Haide Göransson. The girl really wants to stay in the kitchen and help with the sandwiches, but Ricki says she should go and join the others. Her grandparents don't go in for hugging. Shaking hands and giving a little bow is the norm. Grandma has broken her hip and suffered a concussion; she can't walk, and sits in a wheelchair by the window. The girl bows and shakes hands; afterward she wonders whether her grandmother recognized her. Everything is so slow here that it seems to creak a little. Words are like ice floes—not because they are cold, but because no one takes any notice of the water between the floes. Therefore, what is not said is very obvious. She sits straight-backed at a table covered in a sheet of glass, which protects her grandfather's antique coins.

Grandpa is grumpy as usual. And when they are here, Dad is almost as grumpy as Grandpa. Who used to be a professor of electrophysics. When the two of them discuss science, no one else understands a word, and time drags itself along on crutches.

Ricki sits beside Grandma and cuts her sandwich into tiny pieces. She spears them on a fork and holds them up to the wrinkled mouth as if she were feeding a baby bird. Who are Ricki's paternal grandparents? Will the girl ever find out? They come from Småland. They are thrifty. Grandpa is responsible for some important inventions; according to Dad, it's thanks to Grandpa that you can send several telegrams at once. They are distinguished people, she understands that, but their apartment is very small. Even smaller than their place on Siljansvägen.

Grandpa is smoking a cigar in the leather armchair she remembers from Eriksbergsgatan. There was no room for the leather sofa when they moved in here, nor for other pieces of furniture she recalls. Why did they move to such a tiny apartment? Because they didn't want to spend any more money. Because Grandpa is a pensioner now.

They brought their books, of course. Books about mechanics, electromagnetism, physics, telephony, resistance, cable laying, and the theory of relativity, nothing she can read. She occasionally glances over at Ricki, who appears to be encased in plastic when she is here. Ninne is drawing angels on a sheet of paper. Ia is getting fretful; she wants to go home. She sits Ia on her lap even though she is seven years old.

At last it is time to leave.

They bow and shake hands. Ricki comes to the door and waves them off. She really does look like Haide Göransson, although unfortunately she is entirely encased in plastic at the moment.

It has started to rain. Ninne wants to sit in the front with Dad, her hand resting on the steering wheel so she can pretend she's driving. In the backseat Ia falls asleep with her head on the girl's shoulder. Now that they are going to move, she feels as if Ia is the only thing she has left.

And finally: goodbye to her maternal grandparents.

They are very different from her paternal grandparents. They have a market garden close to Lake Mälaren, south of Enköping. The grandchildren spend a lot of time there. Granny is small and dark-skinned, her embrace is soft and generous. However, she can be very strict.

And Granddad is prone to violent outbursts of rage. Everyone must help to pick the crops—the adults are responsible for the apples and plums, the children for the gooseberries and strawberries. They also visit in the school holidays in the winter; it's a bit lonely then, particularly when they are there without their parents. She reads the serials in *Allers* magazine, even though Granny doesn't like it.

And the books on Granny's shelf, especially those by the author who has almost the same first name: Netta Muskett. She writes about daring flying officers, doctors dressed in white, nurses, kisses, and champagne which makes the head spin.

In the summer the steamboat comes, *Ena One* or *Ena Two*, to collect the boxes of fruit for the market in Hötorget. The boat leaves a trail of smoke behind as it plows across the bay. The whistle resonates deep down in the girl's chest.

Everyone runs down to the pier; she is moving so fast that she is flying. Herr Krantz the gardener drives the cart laden with boxes, and dark-skinned Granny runs alongside so that she can add a layer of top-quality strawberries to the punnets at the last minute. The pins fall out of her black bun, strands of hair drift down over her back.

The Dutch are already on the jetty. They are Granny's relatives, and like her they come from Java, where Mom and her brothers were also born. These days the family live in Holland. It's hard to find labor here, and they have no money, so every summer Granddad invites them over to Sweden to pick fruit.

Herr Krantz, with his pipe in his mouth, gets ready to catch the rope. If the boy responsible manages to throw it over the capstan, the Dutch shout *Bravo* and clap their hands. In the summer the long dining table is crowded. Uncles, their wives, cousins. And then the Dutch, chattering away in Dutch and Malaysian.

Long summer evenings, full of talk.

A feast of spicy dishes and homemade ice cream, produced in a special machine on the kitchen steps. That's the way it has always been. But not this time. No Dutch. No one else, apart from them.

It is a harsh, awkward, and sorrowful farewell.

• • •

Childhood is a no-man's-land, although of course I didn't think about it at the time. I didn't know I was in it. The impressions overwhelmed my senses.

The dragonfly on my finger in Granny's rock garden.

The tiny water boatmen, that's what they were called, the insects with spindly legs who could walk on the surface of Lake Mälaren, lifting the water a fraction so that it looked as if they were wearing boots. The cows in the barn, and how I learned to milk them in there, the air thick with dung and hay. The scents of the trees as I ran to the barn, so palpable that I could touch them.

The odor of decay in the potato cellar.

The smell of soap as fru Krantz did the laundry, kneeling on Granny's specially built jetty as she rinsed the clothes in the ice-cold water. And Granny's dresses on the line, all exactly the same, all pinned up by the seams, as if Granny were on display in five different versions of herself.

Now I'm going to talk about something for which I didn't have words back then.

About the fear. About the feeling of being overwhelmed, attacked in fact, by my body. About the loneliness all children share. And about the shadow cast by my parents' dysfunctional marriage. But if they hadn't met, I wouldn't exist.

Some other child, perhaps, but not *me*. That thought crossed my mind from time to time when I was growing up, and it was terrifying.

Something happened last night. Soviet bombers tore the sky apart, and German planes were approaching in strict formation. I was dreaming. What actually woke me were claps of thunder out across the Sound, sharp as cannon fire and salvos from a machine gun.

I woke up, and the room was crisscrossed with lightning flashes.

Then suddenly it was pitch dark. The electricity had gone, and I wrapped the blanket around me and groped my way out onto the veranda. A strong wind blew up. The violent storm struck again; the lightning was like something on a stage. The trees shuddered, their tops bowing down, and the waters of the Sound turned white, as if they were covered with ice.

Nature was running amok, directing its full force at me. The enormous pine tree by the veranda fence was doing all it could to attract the attention of the flashes of lightning. One strike and I would be annihilated. Nature wanted to whip me out of my mind. Don't imagine you're anything at all, that was the message.

Rapid changes of light that fooled the eye.

Blidö on the other side of the Sound was obliterated. The storm was majestic, but everything in my life was ridiculous. I myself was null and void. I protested, but some people sometimes fall into a great well of insecurity, due to circumstances. You have to offer resistance, search for whatever is greater than the self. Writing is a way of offering resistance.

You simply have to persist.

I took a deep, deep breath. And the storm moved away, the wind increased, and suddenly rain was hammering down on the veranda. That's when it happened. I was both outside and inside. Right next to something, and far beyond everyday life. In a nothingness that filled me. I recognized it.

It has happened to me before. The first time was in Hökarängen, some time before the move to Lund. Soon she would never see her classmates again. She took off the cardigan Granny had knitted for her and hung it on the hook outside the classroom. That's when it happened.

She was gliding, slipping, and sliding.

Just the way it was for Alice when she stepped through the looking glass. Time was chopped up, places were sliced in half and came together. She knew she was standing in the school corridor. She could see her classmates' hats on the metal hooks. But she wasn't there. Or she was there and somewhere else at the same time. The place where she had been. Or hadn't. It was like a duplication, a kind of reflection. Like a memory of a memory. She no longer existed. Or she existed in everything.

Last night on the veranda I experienced it again. Perhaps life is a round aquarium, where the fish swimming along keep meeting themselves? But these moments are also a blessing. You exist within something greater, you belong to everything.

The phenomenon is known as déjà vu. Nothing can fully explain it.

2

the knife and
a fortune foretold

In life there comes a moment, I think it's unavoidable,
you can't escape it, when you doubt everything:
marriage, friends, particularly the married couple's friends.
Not the child. You never doubt the child.

• • •

The knife was a compulsion in my head. The first time it turned up was on the school bus in Princeton. It flicked out from my seat. It was enormous and razor-sharp and it sliced through everything the blade touched, trees, houses, cars.

Pedestrians were chopped in half, their upper and lower bodies tossed in different directions. Strollers were slit open and babies' heads went bouncing across the street like little balls adorned with woolen hats. It was appalling. *Get your kicks on Route 66.* A jazz song I remember from America.

The knife was with us on the drive to California.

I buried myself in my book to avoid seeing it. The knife was part of my life for a long time. It was only recently that I managed to change it into a fawn, gracefully leaping over the roofs of cars and from tree to tree. Less violent.

A toned-down variation without spilling any blood. In cars. And on train journeys. Even during my Freudian psychoanalysis I never talked about the knife, or even any childhood memories. At the time, in my thirties, I recalled next to nothing from my childhood. On the sofa I spoke only about how little my then husband loved me, and about the fact that I felt weighed down by guilt, although I didn't understand why.

It is through writing that one can begin to remember.

She avoids looking up at the gray door as they leave the apartment on Siljansvägen for the last time. Mom is nervous and stressed. It is a sunny day in August. The main road is narrow, with lots of traffic.

They might be somewhere south of Södertälje when the knife flicks out from her side of the Hanomag. It cleaves through firs and pines, that's bearable. But it also slices off the tops of oncoming cars as if they were soft-boiled eggs.

The car roof is slit open, heads are ripped away from bodies. She closes her eyes, but she can still see what is going on when she hears the swish of the oncoming vehicles. Everything is played out on the inside of her eyelids, as if on a cinema screen. She opens her eyes, the landscape is painted sloppily outside the windshield, the colors smeared across the sky.

She closes her eyes. It is hot and sweaty in the backseat. Ninne and Ia are quarreling, insistently and infuriatingly. Mom turns her head and asks them to shut up for God's sake, tells her to keep them in order. She reads a comic to Ia. Outside the Hanomag a massacre is taking place.

Swish, swish from the oncoming cars.

She knows that the knife is only inside her head, but that doesn't help. In the country when they were saying goodbye, Granny took her to one side and asked her to be nice to Mom. *Not stubborn. Promise.* Anger punched her in the stomach when she heard Granny repeat Mom's words. Everyone has the right to self-defense, doesn't Granny understand that?

But Granny is Mom's permanent defense attorney. She promises to be nice. That is what she intends to be from now on. She will be as nice as three Pollyannas. But the car journey is going to take two days. She doesn't know how she is going to survive.

They stay overnight in a bed-and-breakfast in Ödeshög.

Her parents are allocated a room up in the house. The children are to sleep in a kind of hobby room with a sofa bed and two camp beds, in the company of a surly-looking moose head on the wall.

Ninne is scared of the moose, and wants to go to Mom. That's definitely not happening. Ninne pulls the blanket over her head and sobs, furious and abandoned. Ia wants stories, and she reads aloud until she is hoarse and Ia falls asleep.

You're the eldest, Granny said. You have to set a good example.

The fact that she is the eldest sister, the eldest cousin, sticks in her throat. As usual it is impossible to get to sleep. She pushes open the squeaky basement door and goes up a concrete staircase. Outside it is night. She sits on a garden bench in her pajamas, shivering and listening to the soughing of the leaves and the sound of crickets.

Perhaps she cries a few tears? Absolutely.

She sobs uncontrollably over Granny's unfairness. And formulates her plan for the future in Lund; it is not unlike a pact or a declaration of intent. No one will ever have the opportunity to reproach her again. Not for *one single thing*.

She won't give them the chance. *Never ever.* She will polish her niceness until it shines like a silver crown. She swears that's how it will be. That is her *revenge* for Granny's great unfairness.

Deathly pale roses are listening, along with cow parsley swaying gently in the breeze, and mosquitoes. When she crawls back into the camp bed, the king of the forest is staring gloomily at her. She would like to rip the horrible thing off the wall and throw it outside, to the mosquitoes and ants.

It's a long time since Dad looked at her affectionately and said, *To think I brought you over the bridge.* He was talking about the day he picked up her and Mom from the maternity home in Stockholm where she was born, and it was wartime.

All of that is long gone. Gone, gone.

The second day is worse than the first. It's not because of the knife. Every time Mom sees a car coming toward them, she covers her face with her hands and whimpers, faintly but audibly.

They drive through suburbs and Dad slows down. A church steeple is cloven in two, the roof of a barn is sliced off, and a row of houses is decapitated. He speeds up and Mom carries on in the same way, covering her face and whimpering.

Every time she sees a car coming toward them!

Does she really think Dad would deliberately crash into another vehicle?

She forgets the knife in order to observe Mom. It is a relief to escape the massacre, but it's only because the drama in the front of the car is taking up all her attention. It is like a silent storm.

Mom is making a point. Or being obstructive.

And Dad doesn't say a word. From her place diagonally behind him in the backseat she can see the vein at his temple beginning to swell. That means he's angry. When he's angry, he keeps quiet.

Mom does the opposite, she uses words. But now she is quiet too, apart from the whimpering. Have they quarreled overnight? It looks that way. Mom is trying to make Dad feel guilty. She knows how that feels, and is furious with her mother. She remembers the promise she made to her grandmother, and places her hand on Mom's shoulder.

What are you scared of, Mom?

Fear, Mom says abruptly. Nothing for you to worry about.

Are you scared we're going to crash?

Don't worry about it. It's just my nerves.

She doesn't believe that. She is convinced that Mom wants to make Dad feel guilty about something. They've definitely had a row. When they argue it always starts off with things that seem to make sense — money, moving to a new apartment, having the opportunity to play the piano in peace, tidying things away. Beneath the surface are heavy seas of antagonism. She can't put it into words, but she knows it's true.

In the car on this August day she is sometimes hurled into her father's silent bitterness, and shares his feeling. And sometimes into her mother's terror of the oncoming cars, experiencing with her the collision in which they all die.

Why don't you stop, Dad?

He is normally so attentive, but this time he doesn't answer.

Can't you see Mom's scared?

He isn't listening. He ought to drive Mom to a doctor (or a lunatic asylum, she thinks nastily). But Dad ignores her and remains silent. Ninne and Ia don't notice a thing. During the journey the trial takes place inside her: which of them is in the right? First Dad is in the dock, then Mom.

After all, one of them must be in the right.

They brought a pressure cooker home from America, which was much admired by friends and acquaintances. A pressure cooker has to have an air vent so that the whole thing doesn't explode. For the mechanics of the pressure cooker — sociology and psychology — a safety vent is required, a valve in case the pressure becomes too great.

I remember that car journey to Lund as a pressure cooker drama.

The Hanomag is filled up with gas. She is allowed to borrow the key to the evil-smelling toilet provided for the convenience of drivers. She feels sick. When she tries to throw up, nothing comes — only retching. It is *just her imagination.*

All the time. It's hopeless. She can't judge between them, and so the fault becomes hers. There is no one else to blame. *She is imagining the whole thing.* She alone carries that particular memory of the journey to Lund.

Her recollection does not match the shared family memory as it is later recounted. Lovely summer weather. Candy canes in Gränna. Picnics on sunlit hillsides along the way. Stopping to swim in a lake. Peace and joy.

They reach Helsingborg, where the road runs alongside the water. It is blue, with an indolent swell. Derricks. A strip of land which is Denmark. Soon they will be able to see Lund cathedral, according to Mom, who seems to have woken up. Who will be the first to spot it?

They are drawn into her silly competition, chanting *Cathedral, cathedral,* until its towers appear above the plain like two connected gray index fingers, pointing up at the sky. They drive into Lund in a good mood.

Their new home is far out to the east. In the newly built housing development where they will be living, all the streets have been named after planets — Tellus, Sirius, Neptunus. Their house is part of the universe too; it is on Vintergatan, which is the Swedish name for the Milky Way.

• • •

Outside the red-brick rented house with its white balconies, Lund comes to an end. Looking down from the balcony she sees a farm and a threshing machine. Whirling dust from the seed. Sun haze and gulls. In the distance she can just make out the road to Malmö.

Inside there is a slightly spooky echo.

But Dad is filled with fresh energy. He cracks jokes, tries to dispel the gloom. He knocks up a dividing wall so that Ninne and Ia can each have a separate room. He hammers, whistles, and sings. She is the eldest, so she gets a room of her own.

For the first time in their marriage, her parents are sharing a bedroom; it is one floor up, and is reached via a spiral staircase. The apartment is bigger than the one they left. Five rooms. From now on the kitchen sofa will be a place to sit, nothing more.

A new school. It is called Lund Community Girls' School, but it also has more academic classes for girls. Dad shows her how to get there by bicycle. This is her sixth school year and her sixth encounter with an unknown class.

A hundred steep steps up to the classroom.

Only girls in the whole school. The teachers are all female too. In the doorway she is blinded by the light; the classroom is bathed in sunshine. The other pupils have just been reunited after the summer vacation; the chatter is deafening, and no one notices her. She comes from the capital, but these girls seem *advanced* in a way that is quite alarming.

She keeps her distance.

At recess the others babble about clothes and makeup. About boys. Needlework: they will be making monogrammed aprons. Cookery: how to prepare food, how to manage household finances. She feels the familiar chafing of being an outsider, the gnawed sensation that comes from being painfully compelled to see herself through the eyes of others. That is the worst thing of all.

You are twisted out of yourself, fumbling blindly.

One of the girls in her class is called Eva. She rests her head on her hands and stares at the wall, her back demonstratively turned toward her classmates. Her hair is cut short, exposing a thin neck. When they happen to be walking next to one another down the stairs, she notices that Eva smells strongly of dog. She does indeed have a dog.

Like many of the other girls she is the child of an academic; she no longer needs to feel like an outsider in that respect. But Eva disappears quickly at the end of the school day, presumably to take her dog for a walk. What is it that is so appealing about her? It is the fact that she turns her back on everyone else with such haughtiness.

It speaks of integrity. And loneliness.

She would like to share her own loneliness with Eva. Might she be in love with her? For a while she suspects this might be the case. That's all she needs — to discover that she's abnormal, on top of the other aspects that make her an outsider. She can't afford that.

Therefore she keeps her distance from Eva. She soon works out the social differences within the class: the girls who seem so advanced live in the west of the city. Those are the ones whose company she seeks. Not immediately, but as time goes by she joins them as they hang out in Lund, in desolate wanderings in search of boys. What are we doing tonight? Hanging out. It's absolutely freezing.

Afterward she has to cycle all the way home. It takes forever.

The creature behind the gray metal door makes an attempt to accompany them to Lund. She appears as a shadow, even more emaciated than before. Here there is no door behind which she can live. She did provide company, of a sort.

For a long time. It was a consolation to take her the leftovers and sit on an empty box watching as she gobbled up every scrap. Now the creature must certainly disappear, if she is not to be outflanked by such a pathetic part of herself. Even if she feels lonely, she can no longer occupy herself with imaginary companions.

She is twelve years old, and wants to be grown up. She is implacable, and the creature fades away (but returns in dreams, hammering on the balcony door, starving and carrying a frozen baby; she doesn't open the door).

Her sense of desolation must end. And fortunately she is given something else to think about. They are sitting around the kitchen table when the telephone rings. Dad answers; it's a long-distance call from Grandpa. Ricki has disappeared!

She went abroad on a group holiday. Grandpa didn't like the idea of her traveling alone, and made her promise to send a telegram from every hotel. So far she has done exactly that. Grandpa reads out the telegrams, and Dad repeats them.

At hotel in Paris. Stop. Everything fine. Stop. Ricki.

And from the next city, Lisbon: *Everything fine. Stop. Your obedient daughter.* From Portugal the group was due to sail to the island of Madeira. Over a week has now passed: no telegram. Ricki's disappearance diverts the tension at home, which is a good thing.

But Grandpa's anxiety spreads seismographically, via neural pathways and telephone lines between Stockholm and Lund, and between Lund and Aunt Laura in Gothenburg. She is Dad and Ricki's older sister. Grandpa worked for the Royal Telephone Exchange in the past, and doesn't have the same respect for telephones and telegrams as others do.

He knows the name of the hotel in Funchal, and sends a telegram. No reply. He then calls the travel agency in Stockholm; they know nothing. Grandpa is determined to get to the bottom of the matter. After a while he learns that Ricki is in fact staying at the hotel. Still no telegram. During a further intense interrogation of the travel agent, Grandpa demands that someone check Ricki's room.

It emerges that she hasn't slept there.

Poor Ricki — does she have to account for every move she makes? Mom thinks Grandpa is crazy.

Dad doesn't like any criticism of Grandpa, and demurs. The travel agent gets hold of the Swedish tour guide who is responsible for the group; he assures Grandpa that everything is fine. Travelers are at liberty to choose from a range of excursions. That's what Grandpa tells Aunt Laura.

Who calls Lund to inform Dad that there has still been no word from Ricki. Whereupon Dad calls Grandpa and reiterates that there is probably nothing to worry about. It might be difficult to get in touch from an island in the Atlantic. Everything has an explanation. No cause for concern. However, according to Grandpa, anything could have happened.

Ricki could have broken her leg. Been stricken by sunstroke. Gotten carried away by the Atlantic currents while she was out swimming. Fallen victim to Portuguese bandits. And when the telegram still doesn't arrive, Grandpa suspects that she has been kidnapped by slave traders to be transported to Africa, which isn't all that far from Madeira.

The white slave trade, that's what it's called.

Your father is crazy, Mom says again.

But by now Dad is also beginning to think the situation is a little strange. Ricki is a reliable person. He talks to Aunt Laura, then Grandpa, then Aunt Laura again. It is during this whipped-up telephone frenzy that the subject of fortune-telling is mentioned for the first time. Dad talks about it, but attaches no importance to it. She, on the other hand, takes a very different view. What?! Has Ricki had her fortune told? Really?

When she is home alone, she makes a long-distance call to Gothenburg. Aunt Laura is a little hesitant at first, but then she tells her what she knows.

Yes, Ricki and Lisa went to see a fortune-teller a long time ago. Ricki was told that she would undertake a journey alone, and would fall in love with a dark man. She would part from him, but he would get in touch with her again. She would marry him and give birth to two sons.

This is staggering.

She doesn't know anyone else who has had their fortune told. Ricki must have met the great love of her life on Madeira. She talks excitedly about the prediction at the kitchen table. Dad isn't interested, and Mom thinks that Laura is probably a little crazy too.

But prediction or no prediction, can't Ricki have a little fling in peace, without Grandpa snapping at her heels? That's what Mom thinks. She agrees with Mom, who like her seems to be imagining something erotic and forbidden.

Who can the man be? Is he Portuguese? An Arab sheikh, an American millionaire? Let's not dramatize, Dad says. Typical. The Earth could collide with an asteroid or an undiscovered planet and he would say, Nothing to worry about, let's all calm down.

So Ricki's cool, calm demeanor is no more than a thin veil, concealing passion and adventure. Grandpa knows nothing about such things. Nor does Dad. She cycles to school, her nipples and the bead between her legs burning. Ricki becomes her stand-in for this encounter with Lund. She is swept up in erotic presentiments of skin and melting kisses.

The fortune-telling brings color to the cobblestones, to the square where vegetables are sold, to the gray stone of the cathedral and the red spire of All Saints Church.

Straw-covered wine bottles in the dreary apartment on Banérgatan, emptied and forgotten, pop into her mind. Has Ricki made previous attempts? This time she will succeed. She is together with Ricki, experiencing a love that exceeds anything in Netta Muskett's novels.

Ricki meets a tanned, sinewy shepherd, not unlike Johnny Weissmuller, on a mountain pass. He takes her to his humble abode and lights a fire. The sheep are moving around them. They make love on his sheepskin rugs.

He is a mountaineer. They are sitting on a rocky outcrop; they start chatting, and there is a spark between them. When darkness falls he asks her to stay, and puts up his tent. After a while they crawl into his sleeping bag. They lie in each other's arms. The moonlight casts its glow over the mountains. As dawn breaks, there is the scent of thyme outside the tent.

Or even better: Ricki is sitting on the beach with a book. A man approaches. He is handsome, with melancholy eyes; he is muscular, like Johnny Weissmuller. He stops by her recliner and bows politely. He has noticed her.

So, she is traveling alone? He invites her to supper at his hotel. They dance to a white-clad orchestra on a terrace in the moonlight.

They sip the effervescent drink of love, champagne.

They are overwhelmed by their feelings. As she is, riding along on her bicycle. In the hotel room tall candelabras surround a bed beneath a white canopy and the sea swell roars in the distance and they can wait no longer. *To be continued in the next issue*, as it says in *Allers* magazine. Her fantasies blunt the sharp edges of her encounter with Lund.

Which looks like a stage set. An overpainted facade.

Unfortunately Ricki contacts Grandpa. It has indeed been difficult to send a telegram. She spent a night away from the hotel because she was with a group of tourists who were interested in botany, under the leadership of a local guide, when they were caught out by a storm.

They had to spend the night in a cave up in the mountains. The following morning the storm had passed, and they all trooped down the mountain and back to the hotel. She is just as calm as always. Everything is absolutely fine. Nothing terrible has happened.

She is on her way back to Sweden.

Sleeping in a cave with a group of tourists? An unlikely explanation. Sounds highly improbable. Does anyone really believe her? Grandpa, apparently. And Dad. But Ricki returns to Stockholm and turns her attention to her drawings once more. She herself still doubts that peculiar explanation.

Her fantasies about Ricki and the fortune-teller's prediction continue unabated.

She devours everything she can find about fortune-tellers, clairvoyants, and mediums in magazines like *Vecko-Revyn* and *Fick-journalen*. Mediums are people who can see things that other people can't. They have what is known as a sixth sense.

They can't explain how they know what they know.

Nor can anyone else, but they perceive things that no one else can see. She reads about a medium in Ystad who tipped off the police about where a thief had hidden stolen goods. And about a clairvoyant in Norrland who told them where to find a man wanted for murder. She reads about famous mediums from the past.

Madame Blavatsky. Annie Besant. Madame du Barry and her crystal ball. And Madame Athena in Paris, who read the cards and practiced palmistry. She reads about a man called Blaise Pascal, who believed that life is a dream, and that true reality is when we wake from that dream.

She would like to wake up to a better reality.

She is unhappy with most things, not least with her body. Her ass, which is too big. The cellulite, which can be cured with orange peel. Her hair, which should be washed in boiled chamomile. According to the weekly magazines, every part of her body should be subjected to treatments which she is too lazy to carry out.

But if Ricki has met a man on Madeira, then a little breach into the unknown will open up. She has definitely met someone and fallen in love. Personally, the girl would like everything — school, homework, loneliness — to fall to pieces like a scrap of very old fabric, and for a *completely different* reality to appear. One that is truer.

And much, much bigger.

Life in Lund is gray and depressing. Soon Mom is just as irritable as she was in Årsta. Dad tries to cheer everyone up. After dinner his mouth is full of cheerful exhortations. *If we all rinse our own dinner dishes, someone soon may grant our wishes!*

They rinse their dishes. Then it's homework.

Mom is sitting at the typewriter, smoking frenetically. She wants to write short stories, but is unhappy with what she has produced and rips the paper out of the machine. The best thing is when Mom and Dad go off together to some academic event. Mom checks her appearance in the hallway mirror, trying on dresses and painting her lips.

When they have gone the apartment feels lonely, but better.

Lund is an isolated planet out on the plain. A particular atmosphere under intense pressure. A bell jar placed over impenetrable changes in the weather. Sundays are the worst.

She stays in bed, listening to the cacophony from the cathedral, which makes her feel strangely oppressed. She listens to Mom's impatience as she nags at them: don't waste the whole of Sunday, up you get, please tidy the shoes in the hallway.

Sundays are a persistent headache in her entire body. And they are followed by countless schooldays, chafing at her soul.

• • •

Who was Ricki really? An independent bachelor girl in silk pajamas or a submissive daughter? Much later, after my father's death, I read the family letters.

Most of them were pretty nondescript.

But not Ricki's. They were a joy to read. The characteristic handwriting, angular and easily legible. The tone is frank, expressive, with ironic undertones.

She lives with her parents (until she is over thirty).

After the outbreak of the war she writes to Laura in Gothenburg telling her that there is a special offer for students who would like to subscribe to *Göteborgs Handels- & Sjöfartstidning*. She wants to read what Torgny Segerstedt has to say about Nazism in Germany and the Swedish appeasement policy, so she takes out a subscription.

The price might be reasonable, Grandpa says, but why *that* particular newspaper? Ricki dodges and weaves. She wants to keep herself informed, she replies.

Can't you keep yourself informed by reading *Svenska Dagbladet* and *Nya Dagligt Allehanda*? Those are the newspapers Grandpa reads. Ricki points out that her paper has an excellent crossword. Grandpa, an inveterate crossword solver, concedes. *Now we meet in the hallway, Daddy and I, and exchange a slightly sardonic smile as we pick up our respective newspapers.*

So Grandpa objected to Ricki's paper?

Evidently. He had admired Germany from his early youth — hardly surprising, given his boyhood fascination with galvanism, magnetism, and electricity. He had German colleagues who were famous nuclear physicists. On top of that, there was the natural distrust of a soldier's son toward the Russians.

According to Dad, during the war my grandfather didn't believe the tales of concentration camps and the persecution of Jews. British propaganda, he insisted. Ricki's letters made it clear that Grandma had a different view. Along with her two unmarried sisters, she went to see the play *He Who Sits by the Melting Pot*, by the Danish playwright Kaj Munk. It was performed at the Vasa Theater in 1938, and is about the Germans' treatment of the Jews.

Which is clearly demonstrated on Kristallnacht, the Night of the Long Knives; it upsets Grandma, but the topic is never discussed at home.

Grandma doesn't want to *rock the boat*.

Ricki also writes about Aunt Tutti. She was Grandpa's sister, and an ardent supporter of Hitler and Nazism. When this loud, hearty sister-in-law from Småland comes to visit, Grandma gets a headache.

On one occasion when Grandpa isn't home they are listening to Tutti enthusiastically singing the praises of the Führer. A strong man. Stylish. Sorted out the economy. Able to stand up to the Communists. Exactly the leader Germany needs.

The paean keeps on coming, while Grandma and Ricki look down at their plates in silence. However, Laura is visiting from Gothenburg. She is a member of the Liberal People's

Party and a keen reader of *Handelstidningen*, and she flies into a rage. She slams her fist down on the table and manages to shut Tutti up. That's our brave sister, Ricki writes (to Dad). Was Grandpa really a Nazi sympathizer? It's not impossible. In which case he would have behaved in accordance with his position in society, keeping quiet and maintaining his reserve. What did he think after the war? No one knows.

An unusually long letter from Ricki to Laura, written over the course of several days: it's all about the Nobel Prize being awarded to the nuclear physicist Enrico Fermi in 1938.

Grandpa was a member of the Nobel Prize committee and the secretary of the Academy of Science, so he was probably the one who informed Fermi of the award. Early one icy gray morning in November he and Ricki, who is twenty-three years old, meet Fermi and his wife and children at the central station in Stockholm after their journey from Rome.

Grandpa gives a dinner in his honor at the Academy of Science in Frescati, where they were living at the time. Fermi's wife does not attend. The Nobel Prize winner is a little stiff, according to Ricki, and his mind seems to be elsewhere all the time. After dinner the young people want to dance, and she puts "hot" jazz records on the gramophone. Fermi receives many invitations from the ladies, including Ricki, but remains sitting at the table "like a stuffed shirt."

The occasion turns out to be a welcome opportunity for Fermi to get out of Italy; his wife is Jewish. Grandpa tells Ricki about the escape plan, and gets involved himself. Immediately after the ceremony the family heads for the United States, where Fermi contributes to the development of the atom bomb. This was their very last chance to escape.

This letter reveals nothing about Grandpa's political stance, but Ricki's letters say quite a lot about her. She had definite anti-Nazi views. Quietly and without making a fuss, she did exactly what she wanted to do.

· · ·

She keeps quiet about the fact that her father is a professor. And the fact that her mother is a professional pianist; it could be construed as showing off, although now of course she has classmates whose fathers are also professors, and who don't find it in the least unusual.

However, just as when she was living in Årsta, she doesn't want to appear to be showing off.

She would prefer not to be noticed at all. That's the way things are for a long time.

She looks up *professor* in the Swedish encyclopedia; it means academic teacher, and comes from a Latin word which means *to explain. No person should be designated a professor unless his skills are apparent and he is regarded as being more worthy of this office than any other man who might be considered.*

It sounds amazing; she feels quite proud. More worthy than any other man. That's true. Professors are men. She's never heard of a female professor. There are women who are married to professors, like Mom. In Årsta no one even knew what a professor was. In Lund everyone knows, and it's the best thing you can possibly be.

Contact with her new classmates, who are trying to be friendly, forces her to produce something new: a clear outline. She has none. Or perhaps she has too many. She is full of disorganized impressions, inexplicable contradictions. Nothing really seems to settle within her.

You are dragged along to something new, released, and expected to swim off into the unknown like a cheerful fish. But that's not the way it is. She isn't cheerful in the least.

And the professor's daughter? That's not *her*.

There is a male physics teacher in school. On one occasion he brings a dead frog to the lab. He sends an electric current through its body; they all stand around watching the dead limbs twitch and jerk. That's what she feels like for a long time: *a galvanized frog*.

Dad might be a professor, but he's not exactly distinguished.

He often behaves like a little boy, farting shamelessly in front of his daughters (Mom never does). He wanders around in the nude at home, completely unembarrassed (such a thing would never cross Mom's mind). He sits hunched in his chair at the table, hearing and seeing nothing. Then he gets up and absently undoes his belt. His trousers drop to the floor and he distractedly steps out of them. They lie there like an abandoned figure eight. Mom shakes her head when she sees them.

But unlike Mom, Dad has a great deal of patience.

When he's around, everything is as it should be. Each of his daughters believes that she is the most loved. He envelops all three of them in his warmth. He reassures them when they have nightmares. His jokes chase away the horrors. And every morning while Mom is still sleeping, he wakes them with hot chocolate in the kitchen.

His three daughters adore him; they want to be with him all the time, but unfortunately he is usually with his students at the university. When he is at home he sits up late with his math papers, so late that he falls asleep on the couch in the living room. In the morning he says that he didn't want to disturb Mom.

Sometimes the girl wakes up in the middle of the night. She gets out bed, still half asleep, to see where the light is coming from. Dad has nodded off in the living room, his book open on his chest. He sleeps in his underpants.

She notices her father's nocturnal erection, although she doesn't know what it is. Gently she removes the book, covers him with a blanket, and switches off the lamp. Why does he sleep on the couch and not in his bed? Because he is *absentminded*.

That's what Mom says: For God's sake, don't be so absentminded!

This is a distinguishing characteristic of professors.

One evening during the first winter in Lund, they are visited by a middle-aged couple. When Dad says who the man is, her memory unfolds like a crumpled-up paper bag: Uncle Bertil! The family doctor, who used to hum hit songs while examining a sore throat.

That was during their previous stay in Lund, and now Dad has bumped into him in the street. He lives not far from the Mathematics Department. He is going to let Dad keep the Hanomag in an outbuilding on their property. His wife's name is Vibeke.

She is statuesque, and speaks with an attractive Skåne accent. She has an infectious laugh. When Dad found out she was a singer who gave concerts and performed in churches, he invited them home on the spur of the moment, hoping to cheer Mom up; she misses contact with the world of music. Bottles appear on the kitchen table.

Dad stands by the stove frying eggs. Although he will soon be forty, he is as excited as a little boy. They drink schnapps, and bursts of laughter fill the air. When she has gone to bed — her room is right next door to the kitchen — it is impossible to sleep. She tiptoes back in her pajamas; she can hardly see anyone through the clouds of smoke. But Vibeke notices her and waves: come and join us, come on in!

She and Bertil are not part of the stiff, academic side of Lund, but the other side: bohemian, cheerful, prone to undergraduate humor.

That's what her parents say afterward.

They are adults — Uncle Bertil and Aunt Vibeke also have quite grown-up children — but they love exchanging banter and pretending to be young. They have joy within them. Which breeds more joy and takes the sting out of Mom's tendency to gloominess. In their company the words fly around like shuttlecocks, the jokes bounce back and forth and nothing is really serious.

Her parents often visit their new friends, where they drink and dance. Even Mom dances, in spite of her lame leg. It is a new time, less rigid and more liberated (this was in the early 1950s, the borders were open once more, the war seemed like a distant memory, and strict morality was loosening up).

On one occasion when Aunt Vibeke and Uncle Bertil are visiting, Mom comes out with the statement that women aren't good enough to be composers. They are only capable of interpreting men's work, she claims angrily.

Mom has a sharp tongue, and likes to say things that wind up other people. Once again it's all about the inferiority of women.

She saw through her mom a long time ago. Mom says this stuff because she wants to be contradicted, which is why she keeps repeating that she is worthless and hasn't succeeded at anything, just so that others will find what she says unreasonable, and object.

You have to contradict her. If you can find the energy.

And indeed the adults in the kitchen protest, Aunt Vibeke most vociferously: Don't be stupid, that's not true at all! Mom comes right back at her: *Okay, name me one significant female composer!* They can't do it, even though they try very hard. Consternation and silence follow.

But the discussion ends in laughter when Bertil remarks dryly that most men aren't composers either; he himself would never dream of pursuing such a career. So exhausting, for God's sake. Even Mom joins in the hilarity.

Presumably Mom thinks men have better opportunities than women. She could well be right, but she tries to get her point across in the wrong way: by angrily and obstinately insisting that men are superior to women.

Just because of their gender. Is she serious?

If she *doesn't* think that, then surely she ought to defend women and say they're just as good as men, if only they get the chance to prove it. It's difficult, because Mom doesn't speak with clarity; instead she wraps everything in her anger.

The girl hasn't given the matter much thought. She can't see any reason why one gender should be better than the other.

For example, how many times has Mom laughed at Dad and told him he's totally tone deaf? Which means that she thinks she's superior to him on that point.

A memory pops into her mind from their previous stay in Lund.

Mom is sitting at the piano, while she herself is a little girl, standing in the doorway on Sandgatan listening. What is a note? Mom asks. Dad replies that a note consists of vibrations. He offers to calculate the intervals between the notes for her, and fetches his slide rule. Mom is furious.

If anything is vibrating it's inside the heart! That's entirely possible, Dad replies patiently, but a note is also a certain number of vibrations. He fiddles with the slide rule as Mom stares at him. *You're completely tone deaf!*

With that she leaps up from the piano stool and leaves the room.

Words are elusive and create misunderstandings. She thinks a great deal about how words and language (and men and women) go together. And why there are no female composers, of course. Is that true?

Mom is emotions and outbursts. Dad is objectivity and calm. Music and mathematics seem to be two opposing languages. Music is female, mathematics male. Most things seem to be either male or female.

What gender are fortune-telling and magic?

• • •

Mom and Vibeke become friends. They both agree that their husbands lack musicality and are tone deaf. They listen to phonograph records together; not just Bach and Beethoven, but also jazz and blues. Mom doesn't like bebop and Charlie Parker — too chaotic.

But Vibeke does.

She turns up with sheet music and sings George Gershwin, while Mom accompanies her on the piano. It is early summer. The balcony door is ajar, the curtains fluttering gently in the breeze, little gusts that make it come alive. The girl is sitting in the corner of the sofa. Aunt Vibeke's alto voice is as soft as cotton.

Summertime, and the livin' is easy. The melody dips its wings in the darkness and soars like a bird. *Oh, your daddy's rich and your ma is good-lookin' so hush little baby, don't you cry.* It is a lullaby for a small child. The women at the piano are tall and dark and in total agreement. *There's a-nothin' can harm you with Daddy and Mammy standin' by.*

It is so wonderful that she is on the verge of tears.

When Mom goes into the kitchen to make coffee, she stays with Aunt Vibeke. I would have liked to pursue a career in singing, trained properly like your mom, Aunt Vibeke says. You must be so proud of her.

The girl has to swallow hard to hold back the tears.

It must be the music.

Or it's because she is proud of her mom.

Mom puts a new record on her new phonograph. The piece is called *Das Lied von der Erde*, by Gustav Mahler, and the singer is Kathleen Ferrier. It is classical music, but this time the shutter inside her ear doesn't come down. The music and the deep voice pour over her. She sees light and shadow, mountains and precipices, colors playing across the surface of the water.

Aunt Vibeke listens with her eyes closed.

Mom stands by the balcony door, gazing silently at the plain. The girl realizes that the language of music captures emotions that simply cannot be expressed in words. Not in mathematics, and not with a slide rule either.

Dad arrives home and is pleased to see Aunt Vibeke. She makes everyone happy; she is as warm as a tiled stove. Mom has finally found a musical friend.

Kathleen Ferrier. Gustav Mahler. She makes a point of remembering the names.

Another memory. Now it is winter. The kitchen table is covered with a stained oilcloth, and the ceiling light has a broken shade. Mom wants them to clear the table.

The girl, on the other hand, wants to talk about the sixth sense. It turns out that Dad knows a professor in Lund who is researching that very subject. She bombards him with questions about the man who is linking science with clairvoyance and the note that is intervals with the note that vibrates inside your heart (and Mom with Dad).

The man is a professor of literature, but he has written books and articles about intuition, telepathy, clairvoyance, and contact with the dead. He calls it parapsychology, and claims that the topic is a huge field of research in the United States.

Dad shakes his head skeptically.

Mom picks up the pot of leftover macaroni and says that when she was young, it was a popular pastime to sit around a table in the dark. A glass would begin to move all by itself, and someone would hear the voice of a dead ancestor.

The voice of someone who's dead! Ninne is all ears.

It was nothing but a parlor trick, Mom snaps.

It turns out that her parents are in total agreement on this point. There is no breach into the unknown. No way out. She stares at the reflection of the ceiling light in the window. What if the mirror image is showing them the way to a more real reality? Dad laughs and says that matter is made up of atoms and elementary particles.

She can hear the shrillness in her voice.

In that case what is God made up of? Is he just particles too?

Dad rinses his plate and doesn't reply, which makes her obstreperous. Surely the five senses can't tell us everything about the world? Why shouldn't mediums and clairvoyants be able to see a reality that is inaccessible to mathematics?

Everyone is entitled to believe what they like. Dad shrugs; he is longing to get back to his math. It is an ordinary evening meal in a Swedish kitchen. The stratosphere is humming, or maybe the sound is inside her head. She can't cope with this literal approach, the urgency, the constant abandonment of everything that is important.

Neither of her parents believes in anything. Life is so blocked up that it is almost unbearable.

• • •

Dad has relatives from Småland living in Lund who are believers. One is even a professor of church history. She can't really say she knows him, but she considers ringing him to ask what *truth* is. She wants to have faith in God, but she doesn't know if she can do that, in all honesty.

One morning all her classmates are hanging out of the window, yelling and whooping. She pushes her way to the front and realizes why.

On the balcony across the street, on the same level as their classroom, a naked man is carrying out his morning exercises. He is jumping up and down, waving his arms. The balcony barely covers his bobbing penis; sometimes it doesn't. She can't believe her eyes. The man is her relative, the professor of church history. Someone is sent to find out who he is, and afterward she hears whispering on the stone stairs: *Ssh, he's her uncle.* He isn't, not literally. She turns and emphatically denies the relationship. Should she call him and ask if God exists?

She dismisses the idea, but not the issue of whether there is a meaning.

The last time they were in Lund, the girls were sent to Sunday school. She held Ninne's hand, proud of the fact that she was allowed to take her little sister without being accompanied by an adult. She was six years old and Ninne was four.

Back home Ninne announced in her bass voice: *Jeeesus can walk on water. Peeeter is an honest man.* Mom and Dad both burst out laughing.

When she was six, she had no doubt about the existence of God. Santa Claus maybe, but not God. Now everything is uncertain. Why do we live? Does she have any value?

In a way that is difficult to explain, the search for truth becomes mixed up with sex. She turns thirteen. Her breasts are large and in the way. She is embarrassed as she hints to Mom — she can't turn to Dad about this — that she needs a bra.

Her mother's gaze is as distant as the Antarctic.

Oh really? Then she forgets about it.

Okay, she was probably busy, sitting at her typewriter, reading the newspaper, doing some sewing. But the fact that Mom forgets is hurtful. She is so deeply wounded that she can't bring the matter up again. She has classmates who are much less developed than her. When they are getting changed for gym she sees their pink and white bras. They already have bras, in spite of the fact that their breasts are smaller than half a plum.

Why them and not her? Presumably because their mothers are interested in them. She thinks her mom dislikes the fact that she now has breasts. That they're already quite large. The craving for a bra takes on epic proportions.

Soon she can think of nothing else.

The bra draws all her sinful thoughts. All her sexual urges. She blushes as soon as she stops outside a shop window displaying ladies' underwear. She edges up to the underwear counter in the EPA department store and picks up socks and vests while wondering if she dare check out the price of bras.

This goes on for months, until she manages to pluck up all her courage. She has seen one that she can afford with her pocket money. What size? How is she supposed to know? The assistant measures her. She can hardly raise her head; her cheeks are bright red, her heart is pounding.

She makes sure the bathroom door is locked before trying on her white, shiny new bra. It fits. She is secretive, hiding it away from Mom, which makes her feel dishonest. Why is this so shameful, so fragile? She feels unseen, neglected, embarrassed.

The wall between her and Mom keeps on getting higher.

Something like that. A crisis of puberty. In an academic's home at a particular time, rational and with a scientific approach. No myths. No faith. The world was flat and without secrets. It hurt. It is clear that Lund, what I saw of it, was a facade, a place where sexuality among modern individuals was regarded as being just as rational as everything else.

No volcanic eruptions. No rivers of lava. But plenty of flirting and laughter among the adults who wanted to keep up with the times. Perhaps it was a reflection of the cultural, radical side of Lund. I didn't understand how lonely we were. Me, us, the city, and the country.

We ignored the things that were important.

My sense of injustice grew.

●　　●　　●

But during the summer after the first year in Lund, Aunt Laura invites her to an island called Origo. Aunt Laura says that she wants to get to know her. She puts on her bra under her dress. Happy to be wearing it. Spends the whole train journey reading. Very aware of her breasts and the bra.

It turns her into a different person, and others look at her in a different way.

Origo is the central point in a system of coordinates. In the universe there are points designated origo, depending on which aspect you choose to study. And Origo is what Aunt Laura and her husband call their island. Laura explained all this over the telephone, and she feels so honored to have been invited that she sees herself as the center of the universe.

As soon as she steps off the train, she can smell salt. They are waiting on the platform, and give her a big hug. Uncle Elis — whom she hasn't met many times — is a small man in a hat with sad eyes.

They drive north in a little Ford Anglia, with Uncle Elis at the wheel.

Aunt Laura rows them across the lake in a skiff they have hidden in the long grass on the shore.

A small grass-covered island in the middle of a lake, a house and a barn. No electricity. No telephone. Laura is nothing like her sister. Ricki is very quiet; Laura talks non-stop. Uncle Elis, on the other hand, is tired and needs to rest. In the evenings when he is sleeping, she and Aunt Laura play canasta and chat.

Does Aunt Laura believe in fortune-tellers?

Laura's hand, holding a card, stops in midair. She replies that she is convinced there are people who can see more deeply than others.

What about the sixth sense? Aunt Laura definitely believes in the sixth sense.

The lights on the mainland are visible on the other side of the lake; a faint mist rises from the water, and as it drifts the shimmering lights sometimes disappear completely. Moths dance toward the windowpane, attracted by the kerosene lamp. Might as well ask.

Does Aunt Laura believe in God?

Yes. Yes, I do.

Even though it is impossible to prove his existence?

Aunt Laura replies that she has no need to prove his existence. Think about it! It is equally impossible to prove that God does *not* exist. An unassailable answer. She is filled with respect. Aunt Laura teaches math and physics. What she says is logical and scientific. Belief is internal.

You have to dare to believe, and Aunt Laura has that courage. It is like Kierkegaard's leap of faith over the seventy thousand fathoms of water (although she has never actually heard of Søren Kierkegaard). A cramp in her belly begins to ease.

Thanks to Laura's talkative nature, she finds out things she would never have known about otherwise. Grandpa was a poor boy who was born in a soldier's cottage in Vimmerby. He graduated from high school and got a job at the Royal Telegraph offices in Stockholm, where Grandma worked as a telephonist.

Grandpa proposed to her over and over again for ten years, and eventually she said yes: she wanted to get married and have children. But then she spent her whole life mourning the fact that she had had to give up work, and no longer had *her own money*. Aunt Laura's voice grows warm when she talks about Grandma. She adds that it's important for a woman to have her own money.

Uncle Elis is also from Småland, and was Grandpa's student at Teknis. He too is a professor — of mechanical engineering at Chalmers Institute. This means that she and Aunt Laura can count at least four professors among their closest relatives. They seem to flourish like mushrooms among the tilled fields and stone walls of Småland.

Laura and Uncle Elis are very fond of one another, but from something that is said she suspects they haven't had much of a sex life due to his frailty, which depresses him. He can spend hours sitting by a play area in Gothenburg, watching the little boys and mourning his lost childhood, according to Laura.

Why does he watch little boys? Is he a pervert? Maybe it's because he and Aunt Laura couldn't have children. One morning when Aunt Laura has gone off in the skiff to buy pastries, she finds Uncle Elis in the dining room. He is wearing a striped robe; he places one hand on the nape of her neck and rests his forehead on hers.

Her breasts, pert in her bra, are pressed against his chest.

They stand like that for a long time. A fly buzzes.

From time to time he lifts his head and gazes into her eyes. His are gray. He sighs. She suspects that something sexual is going on. Is he drawn to children, but can't tell anyone? An alarming thought. She shakes it off. She is the one who is constantly thinking about sex.

All the time. It's manic. Sick. Standing like this with Uncle Elis is not at all unpleasant; in fact it's quite hypnotic. Her head detaches itself from her body and floats around the room like a balloon. Through the window she sees Aunt Laura with a white cake box in the stern of the skiff.

Uncle Elis lets go of her and walks away. This is repeated on one or two occasions. She wonders what it means as she lies in bed with Aunt Laura's paintings on the wall above her. Flowers. And angels. There are also pictures of her, Ninne, and Ia, painted by Laura from photographs. Not angels with wings, but each sitting on a flower of her own. Hers is a daisy.

She looks absolutely ridiculous. Apart from the fact that it's well painted. She feels sorry for Aunt Laura, who can't have children. That must be why Uncle Elis is so melancholy.

They return to Gothenburg. Aunt Laura takes her to the Liseberg amusement park. She wins a big box of chocolates on the Wheel of Fortune and has her photograph taken. Aunt Laura orders a copy. They take a trip on Paddan, the canal boat, and have their photograph taken again.

And as she and Aunt Laura are walking up the Avenue in the fresh, salty air they see — this is amazing! — Birger Malmsten. He is slim and incredibly handsome, wearing dark glasses. He is an actor at the City Theater, and is married to the model and film star Haide Göransson — the woman who looks like Ricki.

She stares after him for a long time after he has passed by. So does Aunt Laura. She has gotten to know her aunt much better, but she will never see Uncle Elis again. He dies shortly after her visit.

• • •

Nothing has changed at home. Aunt Vibeke and Uncle Bertil are visiting; everyone is in the kitchen. Dad is curled up on the sofa with one arm around Vibeke. He is smoking; the hand holding the cigarette is resting on the edge of the sofa.

The other is dangling next to one of Vibeke's large breasts. Her hand is on Dad's thigh, and her head is resting on his shoulder. A bolt of pain shoots through the girl. Dad is pretty drunk, of course, cheerful and red in the face, but how can he do this *in front of Mom*? Vibeke draws him like a magnet.

But how dare they flaunt their attraction to each other when Mom is sitting at the same table? The whole of her teen-age experience tells her: they are in love.

Mom doesn't seem to have noticed anything; she is deep in conversation with Bertil. After a while Dad removes his arm from around Vibeke's shoulders, but her hand remains on his thigh. They are adults. They know what is permissible and what is not. This is just their normal flirtatious behavior.

However, the image of them will not go away. However hard she tries to scrape at it, obliterate it, she can't get rid of it. Did Mom really not *see* what they were doing? Or did she see, and decide to ignore it? She decides to classify the image of Dad and Vibeke as a snapshot. Paste it in a photograph album.

And keep the album firmly closed. That is what she does.

It is time to fill in her application form for high school, and as always she is unsure of herself. She asks her parents for advice. She wasn't expecting this to lead to a quarrel, but their voices grow sharper as they exchange opinions.

She definitely needs to opt for the science route. (says Dad)

Arts — a knowledge of languages is a good thing. (Mom)

She can pick up languages later. (matter-of-fact tone of voice)

Do you think math will make her happy? (sarcastic)

Happy? You're being irrational. The sciences will give her a wider range of career choices after school.

She sits between them in the kitchen, not saying a word. And they keep on going. She tries to work out what it is they disagree about. Personally she would like to leave the room, and the argument. No chance.

Arts, because she's a girl. (Mom)

Gender is irrelevant, science is a way of thinking, you need to start young, otherwise it's too late. (Dad sounds knowledgeable)

You're not listening! (Mom raises her voice)

I am listening, but in this instance I know better. (he's annoyed)

Because I didn't graduate? (a waspish comment from Mom)

It's late, I have to go. (Dad is angry)

As soon as it comes to something important, you take off. (she's furious)

We'll discuss this later.

You need to stay right here until we've finished talking!

Mom rushes after him into the hallway, but the front door has closed and Dad is gone. The argument wasn't about her, it was about something else entirely. All she knows is that she is the catalyst. Afterward she slithers around like a slippery scrap of soap in a soap dish. She chooses the science route, disappointing her mother.

She changes her mind at the last minute and applies for the arts. She is accepted, and Mom is delighted. Why does she drag them in? Over and over again she decides not to let them into her life, certainly not both of them simultaneously.

And then she does it anyway, without thinking. And it always ends up the same way: she is the problem. There is something wrong with her, because she can't please both of them, which is a great source of anguish to her. She senses that the antagonism between her parents lies beneath the surface of the words, deep down in something that is slimy, slippery, and disgusting.

It is something worse than the difference between the languages of mathematics and music. Words cannot be trusted.

If Mom knew what she was up to, she would have good reason to be worried. But Mom doesn't have a clue. They put on makeup, she and her girlfriends; they go to places where there are no parents, and dance in darkened rooms. They make out in armchairs and on sofas. When the light goes on they blink in confusion.

On one occasion a garter belt is lying in the middle of the floor like a dead spider with its legs entangled. Everyone laughs. Until one of the girls, she can't remember which one, grabs the unfortunate spider and stuffs it in her pocket.

She knows the codes. One for the lips, two for the throat, three for the breasts, four for the pussy. Five … but nobody goes that far. Thanks to the codes the girls can quickly swap notes during recess on Monday mornings. She learns the trick of knotting a scarf around her neck to hide the love bites.

When Mom asks what she did on Saturday night, she lies. She doesn't want to be dishonest, but she dare not tell the truth because she is afraid of being hurt, as she was over the business with the bra. Or because she is afraid of something else. Even her own words can't be trusted. She prays to God for forgiveness. She lies in her bed and prays like crazy. It's not the making out, well it's that too, but it's mainly because she isn't being straight with Mom.

It pains her. Other girls have no problem telling lies; what's the matter with her? Why does she find it so difficult? There is something about Mom's life that she is responsible for. What is it? It's the fact that Mom isn't happy with her life. Mom is forced to do a whole lot of things she doesn't want to do. The girl is partly to blame through her very existence.

How can she think that way?

But she does. *God forgive me for who I am.* She wants God to *hear* her, *love* her, and *forgive* her. In bed at night she tries to look up at him. In the darkness she sees nothing but emptiness, a tower of emptiness joined to another and another. She gazes up through all those towers as if she were looking through binoculars.

Emptiness. Particles. Constellations. Distant galaxies. An endless, cold desolation. No room for God there. She turns the darkness-binoculars around. There she is in her bed; she is nothing. Ridiculously imagining that someone who hears prayers in the void actually exists. She abandons her mother by lying.

Personally she has been abandoned by God. Or rather: she doesn't actually know if he exists. She joins her hands on Sunday morning and listens to the church service on the radio; at first she feels pious, but after a while merely hypocritical. It's so boring she could scream. How do they cope, those who believe?

The fact that the universe consists of particles, however, does not prove that God *doesn't* exist. Therefore, she needs to learn about him from those who believe in him. Does she know anyone who falls into that category? Her classmates were confirmed long ago. She signs up for the autumn confirmation classes in the diocese of Lund.

In order to look into the matter. Mom is totally taken aback. *You're going to be confirmed? Right, okay...Why?*

She is perched on Mom's bed in the room at the top of the spiral staircase, and she can't come up with a decent answer. It's complicated. She replies that it's a test. She wants to test herself. And God. Mom becomes pensive; she doesn't say anything nasty, she just says that it doesn't sound like a bad idea.

You're bound to learn something, after all.

Mom adds that she herself would actually like to know too.

This means that the confirmation classes become a kind of project: she has to find out how it all works on behalf of both of them. To find a language where the words are not ambiguous, but clear and direct, so that you are convinced and gain certainty. During the conversation, intimacy grows. Mom, who does everything for them in spite of the fact that she would rather be playing the piano.

Mom, who yearns for so much and also complains about so much. Except for her lameness. And for a moment it is not the girl perched on her mother's bed, but Mom sitting by her bed in the nursery in Lund, reading to her. Mom, who crosses out the word *witch* and writes *old woman* in pencil instead, because the girl is so inexplicably terrified of witches (I notice when I have learned to read). And who says *Momma's angel*, and tucks her in, and everything is fine.

• • •

A miracle happens — Ricki gets engaged! Silence falls around the kitchen table when Dad makes the announcement. That's wonderful, Mom says over the sausages. Who to?

Someone she met on Madeira, apparently.

But isn't it several years since she was there?

It seems they've kept in touch, Dad replies.

And the kitchen practically bursts into flames.

The fortune-teller's predictions are coming true! Her fantasies about Ricki's love affairs were on the money! It turns out that the unknown fortune-teller Ricki consulted could see more clearly than anyone else. This changes everything at a stroke.

If the predictions are coming true, then this is proof that God exists. The world is controlled by an invisible force that operates beneath everything else. She is filled with a sense of reassurance.

Dad is off to Stockholm to meet some colleagues. She wants to go with him, particularly when she hears that the stranger — Ricki's fiancé — is going to be introduced to Grandma and Grandpa. And Dad agrees. He treats her to dinner in the restaurant car on the train.

Who is Ricki's fiancé?

Dad knows nothing, apart from the fact that he's Swedish.

What was he doing on Madeira? Dad has no idea.

Her head is full of questions. Dad has no information about Ricki and her mystery man. She would like to find out a lot of other things. If he is in love with Vibeke. If he's upset because she chose the arts route. If he thinks that God and mathematics don't go together. She swallows her childish questions.

It's a joy just to sit here on her own with Dad. It rarely happens. What mathematical problems are you working on?

She has never asked that before. Dad gazes out of the window and says that he is calculating in an infinite number of dimensions. In n dimensions, where the letter n represents an infinite number. She is totally taken aback.

There's an *infinite* number of dimensions?

Dad replies that there could be dimensions that the human senses cannot perceive, but that in spite of this, math can calculate within these dimensions. They don't really know how it works, but hypothetically, yes. There could be many, many dimensions.

Outside the window hills and houses lurch toward her, and the fir trees pick up their skirts and curtsey. Even though he doesn't know it, Dad has released God from a cramped cage. God rules over a universe made up of an infinite number of dimensions. Sheer excitement makes her a little flirtatious, and Dad seems to like it.

Back in their railway coach he takes out his math papers, while she buries herself in *Captains Courageous*, by Rudyard Kipling. Dad picked it out of the bookcase when she said she had nothing to read on the train. She reads for the rest of the journey: about the spoiled young rascal Harvey, the son of an American millionaire, who falls overboard from a luxury liner.

He is saved by a little fishing boat called *We're Here*, and has to learn how to behave under the harsh rule of Captain Disko.

It is a world populated solely by men and boys. No women; it's liberating. She wants to avoid thinking about sex. The unbearable Harvey becomes a new person thanks to corporal punishment, discipline, and hard work. If predictions come true, then God exists.

Ricki gives her a big hug. Ricki throws her arms around her, looking absolutely radiant. The fiancé? The girl can't take her eyes off him. His name is Olle, he is tall and skinny and looks a little hungry, and as the fortune-teller predicted, he is dark-haired. He has a cleft chin and bushy eyebrows that meet in the middle.

A rakish appearance. A bit like a pirate.

He shakes hands heartily with everyone.

Even Grandma in her wheelchair, which is difficult, but Olle pats her on the shoulder. Once the introductions are over, the conversation falters. Ricki never says much, and what can they discuss with Olle? Not his job (before the engaged couple arrived, Grandpa had informed the others that he doesn't have one). Not his family (apparently he doesn't have one of those either).

It's always hard work with her paternal grandparents. The words are shoveled back and forth with enormous effort. Grandpa sucks on his cigar. Grandma says nothing. Dad also seems troubled. Aunt Laura, now a widow, is in the kitchen making coffee.

It strikes her that she has never met her paternal grandparents outside the family circle. Now, in the presence of a newcomer, she realizes how closed that circle is; inward-looking, almost impenetrable. There are only two ways to make one's way through the mental terrain. One is to keep quiet, like Ricki.

The other is to fill the air with words, as Laura does. Subdue the silence with chatter, with bubbling, babbling, overwhelming chatter, never leaving a gap. Because Olle is there she is able to pick up the linguistic sociology of her grandparents. In spite of their status they are so socially insecure that it borders on snootiness.

At long last Laura arrives with the coffee tray, bringing with her a long, slightly breathless garland of words. As usual there are reams of apologies, she doesn't have much to offer in the way off coffee and cake, she hopes the Danish pastries from the shop will taste okay, she was going to make cookies but she didn't have time. And with an especially pleading tone of voice directed at Olle: the coffee is probably unforgivably weak.

Olle takes a sip and replies cheerily that it could have done with a few more beans. Aunt Laura is so taken aback that she actually falls silent for a little while.

No, Olle doesn't have a job (he mentions it himself).

It's not a problem; he keeps himself busy with all kinds of things. He has spent the last few years living in the Canaries selling underwear — wonderful climate. Everything will be fine, there's nothing to worry about now he has his Ricki. His voice is full of trust.

When the engaged couple have left, she bends over Grandma with her white hair, Grandma, whose expression usually seems lost in the mist.

Did you like him? Grandma asks.

Very much, she replies firmly.

Grandma shakes her head. She much preferred Elis, she says, her gaze sliding out of the window. The ladies' underwear salesman, that's what Grandpa calls Olle. That's when she realizes that Olle hasn't been a hit. It's almost as if it was preordained that her grandparents would dislike Ricki's fiancé.

On the way home she asks if the family aren't pleased that Ricki has finally found a man to love. Dad is sleepy. Ricki will probably end up supporting Olle.

Or your grandfather will, he says.

●　　●　　●

Mom's suggestion sounds innocent at first: why not send their eldest daughter to a language course in Lübeck next spring? It's not far away — just across the Baltic Sea. Dad is busy filling in forms before his departure to the United States. He gathers them up and says that he thinks it's unnecessary.

He never went on any language courses.

Nor did his sisters. It hasn't done any of them any harm.

The idea of a language course seems to him excessive, and would involve a considerable financial investment. Mom stands at the table with the prospectus in her hand, insisting that it won't be expensive. The student stays with a family, the West Germans are happy to welcome Swedish teenagers, it will cost little more than her food and travel. Mom thinks it's definitely worth the money.

She is nailed to the spot between them.

It's about money again.

Dad is thrifty, like Grandma and Grandpa. Mom is frivolous and wasteful. She tries to speak up, tell them she isn't bothered about the language course, but they're not listening. Mom begs, Dad shuts her down. Mom adopts that sarcastic tone of voice. Dad prepares to leave, but stays anyway.

It turns into an exchange of views worse than anything she has experienced in the past. It's not about Lübeck. Or the money. They are arguing about something else. Maybe it's because Dad is going to the States? It's definitely something. She can't work out what it is, but they are gripping each other tightly like octopuses deep in the ocean. As she listens to them, she suddenly realizes: *she costs money*. She hasn't really thought about that before.

Eventually Dad has had enough: let her go, for God's sake.

He flies to the United States. Mom and Vibeke go with him to Kastrup. In spite of the fact that Vibeke is pregnant, she drives them in Bertil's great big Chevy. They take the car ferry from Limhamn to Denmark, and wave him off together. He is going to do research and give lectures, and he will be away for a long time.

I cost money, I am a burden. A horrifying thought. Repulsive. During the winter in the first year at high school it weighs down on her like a nightmare; yes, really, like a nightmare: *the fact that she costs money.* She swears to herself that she will never again accept money at home. She will eat and live there, but she will take care of the rest herself. A firm decision.

She keeps her vow throughout her time in school. There is nothing magnanimous about her resolve; she wants to get away from them, not to be a victim of their obscure, opaque antagonism.

She cycles to the Cathedral School beneath trees blazing in shades of red and fiery yellow, farther on over slippery leaves, her ears filled with the sound of cars swishing along the wet road.

In her head: constant fantasies. A woman in black on the edge of an abyss, the wind tearing at her full-length dress. She steps forward as if she were in an opera (though she has never been to an opera). She calls out, but it is impossible to make out the words.

The woman is magnificent and tragic. She bears a certain resemblance to Mom, but she is more like Cassandra, a famous prophetess from the olden days. She has read about her.

Her tragedy was that her predictions were always correct, but she was never believed.

Evil gusts of wind blow off the plain. Her gloves don't help at all. She bought the cheapest pair available at the EPA department store. Her fingers are so stiff with cold that they could easily be snapped in two.

She cycles with her head down against the wind.

Always late, only just in time for morning prayers. Across the railway line where the farmers transport their beet crops, past the school for the deaf, past Spyken, then the traffic gets heavier. She turns into Södergatan and ends up in a swarm of bicycles and cars. The woman in black withdraws.

She usually makes it before they lock the iron gates. If you're late you get a black mark. Her lungs are burning as she parks her bicycle and races up the stairs to morning prayers.

One winter morning a girl she doesn't know cycles up beside her. She has a pale, slightly doughy face, thick glasses, and a knitted hat.

Her name is Nanna, she says.

Her voice sounds a little muffled as she claims that they attend the same school; she is in the same year, but in a parallel class. They live in the same apartment block on Vintergatan.

She has never seen this girl before. She notices her fantastic woolly gloves, the border of knitted reindeer around her hat. Do they really live in the same building? Nanna moves ahead of her, and she can see Nanna's blond hair sticking out from under her hat, tumbling down over her collar.

Nanna soon changes her mind and slows down. They don't really have anything to say to each other, so she gives her a brief nod and overtakes her. At which point Nanna speeds up and passes ahead.

Then slows down as if she had suddenly thought of something. She overtakes her again. Nanna speeds up again and passes her. This goes on all the way to school. From above they must look like two knots in an elastic band that is constantly being stretched and released. They go faster and faster. This is no longer a bicycle ride, it is a sprint.

Through the narrow confines of Mårtensgatan. Past the square and down Södergatan at breakneck speed.

Two idiots attached to an elastic band. However, it does mean she gets to school in plenty of time. She forgets Nanna and hurries up to the hall, where the principal is sitting jingling his keys as usual. The Religious Education teacher stands on the podium, clears his throat. She tries to breathe some feeling into her frozen fingers. From the stage the asthmatic organ wheezes into life.

Later on she sees the girl called Nanna in the schoolyard. She is alone. Standing up straight, her eyes fixed on a book. All the others, herself included, are surrounded by bodies, chatter, intimacy. Nanna is so alone that it hurts. Such immense lone-liness is hard to see. She turns her head away.

Mom is very busy in Dad's absence. She gets a job with the Scandinavian Youth Orchestra, and she also becomes an accompanist to the cathedral choir. She starts translating a children's book from her mother tongue.

And then of course she has to fix broken bicycle locks, know where the bicycle pump is, take Ninne and Ia to school, do all the things Dad used to take care of, plus she has to shop and cook and mend their clothes. She buys an electric sewing machine which is called Elna and can do zigzag stitching; this makes it easier to turn up hems and sort out buttonholes. She complains that she doesn't have time to do what she wants to do.

Ninne is constantly practicing on her screechy violin. Ia brings home her giggling girlfriends. In order to relax, Mom cycles up to see Vibeke and Bertil, where she admires the new baby, their fourth, an afterthought. A lovely little boy, Mom says, and supplies Dad with his measurements so that he can send over American baby clothes, which he does.

Mom types a letter to Dad almost every day on thin airmail paper. Next to the typewriter are car brochures — Volvo, Saab, Ford. Mom wants a new car when Dad comes home. She is desperate to get out and about! She is going to learn to drive.

Denmark, Germany, maybe even farther.

The Hanomag has had its day. Bertil wants to sell their old Chevy, but Mom writes to Dad that they ought to buy a new car; it's more economical, according to the experts at Saab-Ana. She stays up late, working on her translation from Dutch. In the morning the ashtray by the typewriter is overflowing.

You three must write to Dad too, she keeps on saying. They do, they write to Dad. Her letters are dull. She misses Dad, but she lacks the words to convey what is happening to her.

Confirmation classes. She had hoped to receive guidance about what lies beyond anything that can be proved. It starts badly. The participants are almost exclusively girls, most of whom are younger than her, childish and superficial. The jovial priest who is giving the classes doesn't seem to be taking the subject of faith very seriously.

The catechism. No explanations. Hymn singing.

Can any of you play the piano?

A number of hands are raised, hers with a certain amount of hesitation.

Mom found her a piano teacher, she has practiced boring Czerny-Kretschmer scales without success. She wants answers to important questions, but there is no reference to such matters. And what if one has doubts? One day she dares to ask. The priest stares at her blankly, uncomprehending.

You must pray. God hears your prayers.

Does he? The priest is counting on the fact that they all believe, that their faith is self-evident and unquestioning. How can he make that assumption? He is good-humored, stitched into his priestly role as if it were a coat. His body reveals that he likes good food.

Apparently he is a member of Parliament for the right. Can he, so immersed in worldly concerns, lead her toward the faith for which she thirsts? She doubts it. She also begins to doubt whether the priest truly believes, rather than merely doing so out of habit.

God doesn't get in touch. She had hoped that he would make his presence known in one way or another, but there is no sign of him. On the day when it is her turn to play the piano, she is paralyzed. She lies on her bed, incapable of getting up to practice. The minutes pass, marking time like evil hammer blows. At the last second she leaps onto her bicycle.

She sits at the keyboard staring at the notes, unable to read them.

The very first chord is a disaster.

The priest tells her to go back to her seat. The smell of wet wool is all-pervasive. He plays the hymn himself, leading the singing with a voice filled with iron ore. No doubt he thinks she hadn't done enough preparation. She agrees with him. But there is a resistance within her, tough, unyielding, stubborn, stronger than her.

She isn't asking for much, she just wants the priest to take her question seriously. And, of course, for God to get in touch.

Send a small sign of mutual understanding, a little wink at least. If he exists, as she feverishly hopes he does, then it's really not fair if he speaks only to those who already believe. How are those who doubt supposed to gain access to the community?

Through a revelation. Just like when Saul was cast to the ground and became Paul. Or when Doubting Thomas was told to insert his hand in Jesus's side to feel the wound for himself. She certainly isn't demanding such irrefutable proof, just an internal tremble that would shake her logic, her sensible approach.

A very small revelation, however modest. But the winter passes, and nothing happens.

The fortune-teller's prediction, however, continues to be fulfilled. Ricki gives birth to a son after a difficult labor. A fortune-teller is more reliable than God. She has her doubts about him. She also has doubts about her doubts. Why won't God send her a sign?

She decides it is because she is unworthy.

The fault lies with her again; it is difficult to bear. *If God exists, then in his eyes she is unworthy.* It is an attempt to save her faith from the doubt. And she gets caught up in the idea of her own unworthiness as if she had stumbled into a patch of vicious thistles.

Mom is beside herself when she comes home from visiting Bertil and Vibeke. It has nothing to do with the new baby or the Chevy; it's something Vibeke said.

It's a shame he's feeling so bad, that's what Vibeke said.

So Vibeke and Bertil know better than she does how Dad is feeling? Mom felt like an idiot. The fact that Dad writes to their friends is fine, but how can he open his heart to them and not to her?!

He hasn't said a word to her about how he's feeling deep down. His letters to Mom are sober and trivial. He writes about the lectures he gives, the people he meets, the occasional greeting from a mutual acquaintance. Nothing about deep down. Not a squeak about his innermost feelings. And now she has to hear it from outsiders! Mom stares out of the window as her cigarette sits on the ashtray, smoking itself. What can she say to her mother?

When Dad is away, Mom's moods flow straight into her. It's almost unbearable. It might not be Mom's fault, but it's still really hard to cope with.

• • •

She wants to get out. Get away. She thunders down the stairs heading toward Moonlight Serenade, American Patrol, and the painfully raw sound of the saxophone in Flamingo.

It's Saturday night and Nanna opens her door on the ground floor as she is passing by. Nanna's loneliness is painful. The girl hasn't exactly made an effort to disperse it.

Where are you going? Nanna wants to know.

She answers vaguely, Out, to see some friends. Could she take Nanna with her? This creature with its woolly gloves doesn't fit in, but Nanna is still standing there, and so as not to appear unfriendly, she has to come up with something to say.

How about you — what are you doing tonight?

Nanna replies that she is going to do some reading.

What are you reading?

She asks mainly to round off the conversation, and has already taken a step toward the door when Nanna speaks.

Nietzsche, she says.

And closes her door. Nietzsche! A philosopher, little more than a name as far as she is concerned. So Nanna is reading Nietzsche, even though she's only two years older, according to the school register. That shuts her up. Serves her right. Instead of acquiring knowledge on important matters, she is heading out. Cheek to cheek. That familiar bulge nudging against her stomach.

She is thoughtless. Flighty. Ignorant. She cycles into town, drowning in the heaving seas of her unworthiness.

Britten's mom is out, and the room where they are dancing is so small that they are all crammed together. I Cover the Waterfront. A Night in Tunisia. Mouths and bodies. A herd of buffalo. Everyone's arms are warm. Stan Getz. Dizzy Gillespie.

She dances with Svante, she hugs Britten, Svenne kisses her, and Robban places a hand on her bra, sending electric currents from her nipple straight down into her clitoris. And Britten's mom arrives home a little the worse for wear with a guy who is a poet, apparently. They drink wine in the kitchen, where Britten's mom sleeps.

They carry on dancing, until Britten's mom appears in the doorway.

I know you're having fun, boys and girls, but it's time to call it a night.

The closer she gets to home, the more guilty she feels. It's the making out, it's Nietzsche, it's the knowledge that she's unworthy, and it's Mom.

In the end she has to get off her bicycle.

She stands there puffing and panting on Dalbyvägen.

Her conscience refuses to be assuaged. The clouds pass by on their way to Africa. The bushes along the cycle track point at her with accusing branches. Over by the railway line the only lamppost looms like an emaciated ascetic. *Unworthy, unworthy,* everything around her is calling.

In the early spring she comes home from her confirmation class, nothing going on inside her head, and pushes her bicycle into the rack. She lifts her bag off the parcel shelf and drops it with a crash. She looks up at the sky.

Above the apartment block next door, separated from theirs by a frost-covered lawn, a thin white moon is hovering, veils of cloud wrapping it in a cozy blanket.

The clouds thicken and disperse, and behind them the sky is as blue as a sapphire. The moon looks like a bird's egg. The bird's nest drifts down toward the earth. All is peaceful. There has been nothing but noise since they came to Lund. Constant attempts to be attentive, to take note, to fit in. And beneath it all the ever-present anxiety: how is Mom feeling?

Now, for example. She ought to go up and see her.

But she stays where she is. God doesn't contact her, but still she stands there, happily liberated from her thoughts for a while. It is an unexpected interlude of peace.

Then she picks up her bag, pushes open the door, and switches on the light. At that very moment Nanna opens her door, her fair hair curling around her shoulders, glasses shining. She is wearing a bulky sweater and wide, airy pants. Her dog, a black poodle, is winding itself around her legs.

And Nanna asks, Where have you been?

She answers truthfully. At her confirmation class.

Everything changes in an instant. Nanna's posture, the look on her face, her voice. It is no longer muffled, but shrill and accusatory.

You mean you're going to be confirmed?

That's the plan, yes.

A torrent of words comes pouring out of Nanna. She hasn't been baptized, therefore the church will not allow her to be confirmed. She doesn't want to be, anyway. Priests are hypocrites. Just like missionaries. They frighten the poor natives, whom they call heathens, telling them that they will burn in hell unless they are baptized, they force them to undergo baptism. That's how they prepare the way for soldiers with cannons and rifles, and for white colonialists. That's what Christianity does.

You do realize you share the guilt if you're confirmed?

I hadn't realized that, no.

The bulb in the stairwell goes out. Nanna switches it back on. The light is cold and harsh, and Nanna's fury seems to be increasing. Don't you realize that the church claims that I will burn in the fires of hell, simply because I haven't been baptized?

Oh come on, don't take it so literally.

It's in the hymnal. You're going to be confirmed, and you haven't read it?

No, I haven't, and I don't believe that's what it says.

In that case I'll show you, in black and white!

Nanna disappears into her apartment. The dog trots after her, the sound of its barking echoing in the stairwell. Why is she still standing here? Because she is paralyzed by her bottomless ignorance. She has no idea how the church feels about those who haven't been baptized, Jews, Mohammedans, and atheists. Nor can she rule out the possibility that Nanna might be right. To her, God is a promise that life isn't meaningless. She can't come out with something that simplistic.

And she wants to keep her own uncertainty about him to herself.

But Nanna is back, waving the hymnal. The fine print flickers, and she can't read the words. She is seized by panic. She tumbles out of herself, out of the fragile protective shell that holds her together if need be. It is as if her intestines have fallen out, as if her innards have been exposed in front of everyone. She doesn't know how she manages to get up the stairs.

But from that moment she fears Nanna.

It is an irrational, senseless, paralyzing fear.

The lonely girl on the ground floor, who was perfectly harmless to begin with, is transformed into an internal accuser, an all-seeing eye that persecutes her. Nanna can observe everything from her kitchen window. When she gets home. When she cycles into town with her burning pussy. Who drops by to visit.

Nanna can open her door and ask questions at any moment.

Questions the girl cannot answer.

She is going to be confirmed, but she hasn't read those words in fine print, the terms and conditions of the contract she has apparently signed, and for which she can now be held responsible. Even though she still isn't sure whether God exists!

As usual she has been less than conscientious. And the presence of Nanna in the building — what evil power made them neighbors? — forces her to admit that everything within her is resting on far from solid ground. She knows nothing, can achieve nothing. She is intending to be confirmed, in spite of her doubts. She is driven by sex. She lies to her mother.

Nanna can see right through her, deep inside her. Nanna knows she is not the person she pretends to be. This causes panic, a headlong tumult. After this encounter she does everything she can to avoid bumping into her neighbor. In the mornings she closes her own front door behind her, then stands and listens, her heart pounding with fear. Has Nanna already left?

Or is there a danger she might meet her horrifying accuser? She bends double, panting with terror.

Then she hurtles down the stairs, slipping and stumbling, her schoolbag catching on the handrail until she manages to throw herself onto her bicycle.

•   •   •

What forces did Nanna trigger within me? We hardly got to know each other at all during those four years at high school. She would occasionally come up to our apartment to ask about something, a test or a sports day.

I answered politely, but never invited her in.

I was vaguely aware that I was projecting dark thoughts onto her. It didn't help. Although I was afraid of her, at the same time I couldn't help feeling sympathy for her. Nanna and her mother on the ground floor *were* very lonely.

It was the same as with Mom: feeling sorry for someone, while simultaneously being scared of them.

Perhaps it was that particular combination that I couldn't cope with. Nanna became a menacing wedge in my all-too-unstable mind.

A hell of a pain in my ass. During almost the whole of my time at high school I avoided my ground-floor neighbor as best I could. It is one of the most powerful projections I have ever experienced.

All the conflicts within myself that I was unable to resolve — God and Mom, sex and shame over my sexuality — I put down to Nanna's gaze upon me.

Which became horrifically menacing.

When we eventually became close friends in later life, after graduation, I was still a little afraid of her. I was always kind of on my toes with her.

She knows that she is unworthy before God. And then one day Ia comes along with something to tell her. Ia is in the same class as one of Vibeke and Bertil's children, and frequently spends time at their place after school.

One day when they are alone in the kitchen, Ia starts babbling about Dad. Before he went to America, he often used to come around to see Vibeke. He would turn up on his bicycle when Bertil was at work. The children *spied* on them. They saw them *kissing*. They *secretly* read Dad's notes to Vibeke, arranging where to meet.

Don't say anything to Mom. Ia is ten years old, and as excited as a secret agent who has found a hot lead. She wants to know what her big sister thinks. What is she supposed to say to Ia? She replies, sounding as supercilious as she possibly can, that Ia is too little to understand.

If Dad comes to call it's because he and Vibeke are friends. Is there anything wrong with that?

No, Ia says, looking relieved.

If she herself took any notice whatsoever of what Ia said, it is because of her own sordid thoughts. She trusts Dad more than anyone in the world. He isn't exactly God the Father, he's just their dad. She brushes aside her suspicions as one might wave away a persistent fly. She can't talk to anyone about the things that are really bothering her: God and who she actually is.

●　　●　　●

The confirmation service takes place in the cathedral choir. They sit in front of the priest clutching their hymnals. The girls are dressed in white, the boys in suits. Down in the pews relatives and friends and Mom are listening.

Tall candles surround the candidates. The cathedral's pillars shimmer in the candlelight, disappearing in shadows and cobwebs. The priest asks her the question about the Bible stories: Adam and Eve, Moses and the burning bush, the Annunciation.

Can we believe in the miracles in the Bible?

She says firmly that they are not true. The priest stares at her in consternation. She tries to rescue the situation by adding that stories and miracles could perhaps be regarded as symbolic truths. She knows she is on thin ice, but continues to embroider her thought process to the end, not without sophistry.

She is as honest as she can be.

She doesn't participate in the declaration of faith: a slim gesture of integrity. She has not achieved any certainty that God exists. Nor the opposite. The question will just have to remain open for the time being. Perhaps she ought to have opted out of the confirmation service, but she is too much of a coward to do so.

She goes through with it partly to avoid proving the arrogant Nanna right. She wants to keep her uncertainty to herself! It is a free space and it is hers and hers alone.

Maybe the whole thing would have passed off smoothly if Mom hadn't made the confirmation into an event. She invites a number of ladies to the apartment to celebrate; what is there to celebrate? But there is no getting out of it. After all, as Mom points out, she is doing it for *her* sake. How could she tell Mom, who doesn't believe in anything, that she is torn? That she feels as if she is beset by demons?

It doesn't show on the outside. Mom serves coffee and cakes. She receives jewelry and poetry anthologies. Aunt Vibeke gives her Hans Christian Andersen's fairy tales. She says thank you, she smiles. Her skin feels raw, as when a dressing is ripped off a wound, leaving it open.

The wound festers and suppurates. And the next thought: who does she think she is, making such a big deal of herself? Taking herself so seriously — it's absurd! Afterward she pulls off the white dress and goes out.

She is rebelling, and has no one to rebel against. On the way home, when she sees herself from the outside, bent over the handlebars pedaling furiously, she finds herself utterly ridiculous.

She sits down on a beet crate by the railway line and manages a slightly hollow laugh. She has the right to keep quiet about her uncertainty at least. Until she has acquired a skin that is strong enough to hold her together. Then Nanna can sit there in her big wide pants reading Nietzsche as much as she wants.

The great event in the spring when she turns fifteen is not her depressing confirmation, but a performance of the *St. John Passion* in the cathedral.

Sometimes Mom practices at Vibeke's, because Vibeke is breastfeeding her new baby.

Later they rehearse in the cathedral with singers and musicians. Mom is full of praise for Vibeke, who is singing the alto part. She also admires the other soloists and musicians, but is nervous about her own contribution. What if she has a tummy problem, what if she goes wrong, what if she faints?

After all, Mom suffers from *nerves*, as she puts it.

On the evening of the concert she cycles to the cathedral alone. As usual she is late, and the place is packed. She is given a program and sits down on the stone floor with her back against a cold pillar. Johann Sebastian Bach, one of Mom's favorites, gets off to a flying start. It is like a theater.

And it's overwhelming! The power grips her. The melancholy and the tenderness, the rage and the sorrow. And the story: Peter's denial in the courtyard, Pontius Pilate and the trial, the people yelling crucify him, crucify him! And the Roman soldiers who offer him *Essig* when he is thirsty.

Vinegar! Offered up to his cracked lips.

The man on the cross gives up his spirit.

Es ist vollbracht. Vibeke's alto voice conveys deep distress as she repeats those words. Suddenly she realizes that *vollbracht* doesn't mean only death, but completion. Coming home, peace. Soon the dead man will be home with his father. Even though she is sitting on a cold stone floor, she feels a wave of warmth and her eyes fill with tears.

Then it's over. The soloists take their bow. She can see Vibeke, elegant in a black evening gown. She has listened for the harpsichord, and felt proud of Mom, who played all of her sections beautifully. There is no sign of her. Lots of people are unwrapping bouquets of flowers, ready to present them. She never thought about flowers. She stumbles onto the stage. Mom is sitting at the harpsichord, and looks up at her. Those black eyes.

That beautiful, animated face!

At that moment she doesn't see the mom who is so full of contradictions, such hard work; she sees her mom as a person in her own right. And she loves her. She cycles home. It is one of those chilly spring evenings in Lund when the buds are just about to burst into life.

From Copenhagen and the Sound comes a faint hint of the sea. Everything is incomprehensible, everything is fragile. But that evening, cycling home from the *St. John Passion*, she is fulfilled. Uplifted. The world is bathed in a brighter light.

• • •

Many years after the *St. John Passion* in Lund Cathedral I read my mother's letters to my father during his long absence in America.

They were breathless, hectic, cheerful.

Mom was dead by then, and the letters were found among her belongings. I didn't even know they existed, but Ia gave them to me, along with some other papers, when I was visiting. Before her death Mom had stapled together her letters to Dad, written on thin airmail paper.

Lots and lots of staples. As if she had been in a violent rage.

It was almost impossible to remove them without tearing the sheets, but I managed to prise them out and read the letters one night, with mixed feelings. The tone was so forced. So anxious. So many typing errors.

The sentences stumble over one another. Mom has such a lot to do. She writes about her activities at great length. She seems proud of the fact that she is earning money. She misses Dad, although she often expresses herself with a certain sarcasm.

Or rather: with a slightly throwaway, plucky edge.

And yet the tone is warm. Intimate and friendly. Toward the end of spring Dad sends her a nylon blouse, which makes her happy. She writes that the blouse makes her think that she, his old wife, still means something to him.

It seemed to me that they must have had a big discussion before he left; I'm sure she didn't want him to go. That's what I thought.

And that with these letters she was trying to mend something between them. In letter after letter she writes about the new car she wants them to buy when he comes home. She tells him about the *St. John Passion*, how well it went, and how much she appreciated Vibeke's contribution.

It is clear that she didn't have a clue about Dad and Vibeke's relationship.

I reread the letters several times to make sure. I had known for a long time that the affair had started when we arrived in Lund, and had gone on for many years.

But Mom had no idea. They fooled her.

It was heartrending. And what should they have done?

Maybe they were trying to be considerate. The price they had to pay was the lie. Although I was old and they were dead, I sat there with those letters for a long time. It was night. Ia was asleep, and the apartment was silent. When I was little I used to try to console myself with what Dad always said: It won't matter in a hundred years. It was no consolation now. Darling Mom. It hurt to read her letters.

A small town drama from all those years ago, who could possibly care about it after all this time? Who hasn't deceived someone, who hasn't lied? I have. But this was about them, about my parents. A lie has its own anatomy, even when it seems necessary. Even when it is perpetrated out of consideration. It is not possible to carry out a consequential analysis of the lie, it continues to have an effect at the third and fourth remove.

Why did Mom still have the letters? He brought them home from the United States, of course. I guess he didn't take them with him when he left us.

Before her death Mom had gone through her papers carefully; she had thrown a lot of things away. Most things. There are no letters from Dad to her while he was in the States, nor any other letters written by him.

But she kept these letters, the ones she had written to him. I assumed she wanted us to read them. Afterward there were fifteen, twenty bent and twisted staples lying on the table. They looked desolate. I swept them together with my hand.

3

on how you find out

Writing also involves not speaking.

It means being silent.

It means screaming without a sound.

• • •

The thought that *I cost money* was unbearable. I didn't accept any money at home. I worked throughout my time at school. Not accepting money for clothes, trips to the movies, the theater, school dances was the most important decision of my whole life.

Unfortunately my parents didn't notice; they were so preoccupied with themselves.

If I had suffered in the past because I couldn't please both of them, now I felt as if I were being split into several different individuals. Being an unwanted item of expenditure was the blackest. The others were colorless. *I* existed only in the outermost circle of transparency, in the thin invisibility where I was *myself*, and where I tried to preserve my integrity. During Christmas vacation in my first year at high school I sold men's slippers in the EPA department store.

When I came back from the language course in Lübeck, I babysat for a doctor's family. During the rest of my time at school I worked weekends and vacations as a care assistant in a facility for the chronically sick up in the north.

Unfortunately she falls in love. It's before the trip to Lübeck and the language course. It's not the first time, but on this occasion it's as if a crater opens up inside her. The trees are in full leaf. They sit on a sofa kissing with a party going on all around them and Lena Horne singing from the record player:

Love me or leave me and let me be lonely
You won't believe me that I love you only.

They kiss each other at several parties. He plays the trumpet at school dances. He has a red moped, a Mustang; she learns to recognize the sound of it among the hundreds of mopeds in Lund. One afternoon it zooms past the apartment block on Vintergatan and disappears. But it comes back.

And the doorbell rings. She opens the door and he's standing there asking if she'd like to go to the movies. She starts trembling. Mom is playing the piano; she tells her she is going out. Mom lifts her hands off the keys and her voice can be heard all the way out into the hallway: *What on earth's wrong with you, your entire body is shaking!*

Please Mom. Not so loud. Mom takes no notice. In an equally loud voice: *The movies? Absolutely not! You're always running off somewhere or other!*

She goes back to the front door. She can't trust her voice, she can only shake her head. When he has gone she is trembling so hard that she thinks she is going to faint. She sits in her room, her whole body shaking.

After that he doesn't contact her again.

She doesn't see him for a long time. And he doesn't get in touch. She is too proud to make the first move. She travels to Lübeck with Swedish students from all over the country, and she is still in love. For the classes, which are held in a boys' school that is closed for the summer, they read Thomas Mann's

Tonio Kröger. The German is too difficult, but Tonio, with his great sensitivity, becomes a soul mate. The novella is set in Lübeck long before the Allies' bombs fell. At the Marienkirche there is a pile of bricks from the clock tower that crashed to the ground. The signs of war have not yet been cleared away.

The family she is lodging with takes her to Travemünde. She sees the raked sand through binoculars. That is East Germany. She sleeps in a trailer in the family's garden; it was used by refugees during the war. She has read about what life was like in the serial *Child 312* in *Allers* magazine at Granny's house, with illustrations by Ib Thaning, whom she admires. She is trying to learn how to draw from these illustrations.

She is homesick, and Mom's letters are a pinprick of light in the darkness. Her obsession with the boy she loves is driving her crazy; she does everything she can to kill it.

She lies on the grassy bank of the river Trave and kisses a German boy in lederhosen whom she doesn't care about at all, untroubled by her conscience. She learns a great deal during her stay, and not just German. It's her first trip abroad alone, and it turns out to be crucial; she learns such a lot.

About the war, about Europe.

And she is beginning to harden her heart against love. *Die Verhärterung.*

She doesn't know that she is on the way to becoming a person who is difficult to love. On the outside she is happy, always happy. On the inside she is covered in a sheet of ice, and it will cost her an enormous amount to break through.

When she returns home she works for a family in Mellbystrand, looking after the children and helping with the housework, and it doesn't pass. She receives a grant from the King's Fund and travels to Norway, although she has no idea why she has been selected for this honor; she is far from the best in her class.

She is still in love; the feeling does not pass.

It hurts so much that she sits on the floor in a house on Kullen; she wraps her arms around her body and rocks back and forth to ease her pain. This is worse than the sense of loss when the boy with the Mustang dumped her in the first place. This is a deficiency disease over which she has no control. It feels as if nails are being driven into her body.

Kullen: they are there because after his return Dad was allowed to borrow a house that belongs to the university. The family is spending a week there in late summer. To get down to the sea you have to clamber down the cliff using rickety wooden steps, far too unstable for Mom to make it to the water.

The girl climbs down frequently to seek a cooler spot.

And when she reaches the bottom of all those narrow steps there they are, Dad and Vibeke, leaning against the fence with the child between them. Their silhouettes are black against the sparkling water. Yes, Vibeke turns up in the car with her little boy and is warmly welcomed by Mom and Dad.

She walks past them and into the sea. As she swims the water eases her pain for a while. The gulls sail across the sky, and in the distance she can just see Denmark. Her only consolation comes from reading and drawing. She always has her sketchbook with her in her bag. In Germany. In Mellbystrand. In Norway. In the park in Lund, and in the house on Kullen.

People, their faces and bodies. Capturing their contours on paper gives her a feeling of being present. It gives her the sense that she exists, if only as an observer. When she draws she is there and nowhere else.

In the second year at high school they move on from miserable Cicero and meet Catullus. The Latin teacher reads the poems aloud in Swedish before they tackle the original texts. Once again she is reminded of the torments of love. Catullus wanders drunkenly through the alleyways of Rome bellowing the name of his beloved. She doesn't know if she is filling the verses with this unreasonable torture, or if it is there already.

Oh God, surely it must pass eventually?

Yes, with difficulty. Her obsession fades away with a desolate, lingering chord.

Catullus's pain is like that of a woman. But he was a man. He can do whatever he wants, be drunk and crazy one minute, tender and desperate for love the next, at least in his poems. Love, love, love. Hate, love, hate.

Love again. A man doesn't need to be ashamed of his love. She can't afford to behave that way. She is done with love. The only solution: to make herself impenetrable. You can't just let yourself disappear into a sinkhole. You have to draw a line in the sand, build a barrier against this sickness that makes you lose all control.

· · ·

Mom comes into her room. Was it in the autumn of her third year at high school? Something is wrong. Seriously wrong. She looks up from her English grammar and Mom bursts out: *Vibeke can't be trusted — just so you know!*

She walks out of the room with no explanation. Outside a sullen twilight is falling. The penetrating scraping of Ninne's violin can be heard in scratchy, disjointed sequences, punctuated by the sound of Ia's ball thudding against the wall. She can't follow Mom and ask her what she's talking about. Dad is sitting in the dining room, working. Why does Mom feel the need to pass on this information? What is she supposed to do with it?

It's not her problem; she feels a surge of resentment, which leads her to print on the inside cover of her English grammar book: AUNT VIBEKE CAN BE TRUSTED. She reads what she has written from time to time, and there it stays. She can't really explain her reaction, but a family is a communicating vessel. She remembers learning how such a vessel is constructed in Physics in junior high — that and the galvanized frog.

A number of glass tubes are connected to one another.

Liquid is poured into one of them. It spreads throughout the tubes, until the level is the same in all of them. She doesn't want to be affected by Mom's moods. She wants to regard this incident as an outburst brought on by Mom's hysteria.

One night a little while later, after a wild party, she ends up with a guy in the poverty-stricken Nöden district in the middle of Lund. The boy is ugly and clumsy. They go to the same school. It is freezing cold back at his place. No adults. A shabby apartment with the same smell she remembers from Årsta: poverty, lack of hygiene.

They make out. She feels nothing but distaste. She notes his thirst for love.

She lets him keep on, caresses him in return.

The whole thing is tasteless, but she can lend herself out. She almost thinks it's her duty. His hand finds its way inside her panties. He wants more. After a few minutes she removes his hand and leaves. He doesn't protest, he merely looks sad. It is as if she encounters a part of herself in him. Why shouldn't she lend herself out when she sees his loneliness from her distant ring of transparency?

If she were being honest: she went with him because he wasn't dangerous. Because she knew she didn't want him, which gives her the upper hand. The same thing will happen again with others. She doesn't want to be drawn into love. It is too dangerous.

And yet she longs for it, so much that it almost drives her crazy.

A few years later when they are both due to graduate from high school, the boy can't cope. He has to sneak out the back way, like those who fail their exams. It is the memory of this *sneaking out* that came to me when, after many years, I happened to see his death notice in the newspaper. An announcement. No grieving family or friends mentioned beneath his name. So alone, without love.

She has to cycle up a steep hill to get to the facility for the chronically sick. It's hard work on ice-cold winter mornings, but she enjoys the job, it enables her to earn money, and it is an important part of her time at high school. Most of the patients are elderly and suffer from rheumatism; many have multiple sclerosis.

Fröken Gren, for example.

She is a tall woman, her body as stiff as a board, and she is always equally pleasant when she is being washed. Something falls out of her vagina like a fleshy flower. Fröken Gren calls the girl her ray of sunshine; it feels good.

Bad-tempered fröken Nord is a different kettle of fish. Her body is a compact, tangled ball of limbs. She has to be washed, upper and lower body, and different-sized cushions and pillows have to be pushed into hollows and crevices.

And all the time fröken Nord barks like a stray dog. The complex procedure ends with a pointer being inserted under one arm so that she can use it to turn the pages of the magazine on the cushion in front of her.

The only young patient in the facility is Lotta.

Younger than her — only fourteen. Half of Lotta's head is wrapped in bandages; she has a brain tumor, and knows that she is going to die. She has only one eye. The other has been surgically removed. Occasionally one of the local boys offers Lotta a ride on the platform of the moped he uses to make deliveries.

And Lotta, curled up on the platform looking like a little mushroom, turns her one eye up to the treetops and roars as loudly as she can. The boy takes the corners at breakneck speed. The senior nurse, Sister Nelly, stands beside her on the veranda. Her only comment is that it's great for Lotta to experience some happiness during her short life. Not a word about recklessness.

An elderly woman from one of the villages outside Lund has a cannula in her throat, and is unable to produce any comprehensible sounds. She is small, with curly gray hair, and no doubt she was once beautiful. Her eyes are naked and despairing.

She writes little notes, begging to be allowed to die. One Sunday the time comes, and the family gathers around her bed. They are dressed in black, singing hymns and sobbing. Against all expectation, the woman survives. Sister Nelly calls the girl to her office. And yes, she admits that she gave the patient all of her countless pills at once; she didn't realize they were supposed to be spread throughout the day.

Sister Nelly sighs and says let's forget about this, let's not mention it to anyone. She obeys Sister Nelly, she forgets about it and is grateful. And a little more hardened; best to delete the fact that she practically killed the old woman.

Once upon a time death was incomprehensible. A dead hare in a field, small and shriveled. A swarm of flies rose from the body as she and Dad approached. The knowledge that life departs like a puff of steam is hard to grasp.

But at the care facility, people die. One after another. The bodies are taken away on gurneys at night to avoid upsetting anyone else. If it's a general ward, they wheel out the bed. Fru Asplund, however, has a single room, and the body can be washed during the day.

She stands by the bed with fru Jönsson, who is a care assistant. Fru Jönsson is used to this, but for her it is the first time. She has washed the living fru Asplund, who was a big woman, many times. Chatted, helped out at mealtimes. Now she and Jönsson are standing here, each with an aluminum bowl, a bar of soap, and a washcloth.

They pull back the sheets and see that the deceased has soiled herself. That often happens at the moment of death, Jönsson says in a matter-of-fact tone as she drops the nightgown and sheet on the floor. They wash the body from their respective sides.

They turn it over and wash every nook and cranny. The body is dead, but still warm. The whole thing feels very strange. At last the deceased is clean and tidy. Her hair has been combed, she is wearing a clean white nightgown and her hands are folded on her chest. Jönsson calls the porter, who brings a gurney. Together they transfer the deceased.

It is her job to clean the room while the deceased is still there: bedside table, closet, floor. She talks nonstop, directing her comments to the deceased: *It's fine, you've passed over, have a good trip, it was lovely to meet you.* Death is frightening and she is trying to get used to it. To become hardened to it.

In the evening the porter returns and removes the body. There is a mortuary down in the basement. No doubt it is made to look like a chapel.

She never visits that room.

• • •

Grandma dies too. They wander around the Northern Grave-yard, Grandpa, Aunt Laura, Dad, and the girl, unable to find the grave site. It is pouring with rain. Ricki and Olle aren't there; they are at home with their little boy. Grandma has been cremated, she has been licked by flames, bitten by fire. What remains is ash and fragments of bone. Is she mourning her grandmother?

It is impossible to mourn a shadow. The rain finds its way down inside her collar. Her hair is sodden. Grandpa is wearing a black hat. Aunt Laura has pulled a plastic rain hood over her hair, and Dad is in his pale American suit. *Here!* Aunt Laura shouts, but she is mistaken.

Apparently it's a family grave. She's never seen it.

Here! Laura tries again, but once again she is wrong. Grandpa looks unexpectedly small in his black coat. Rain is dripping off the brim of his hat.

A green spider — actually it's a man on a bicycle in a green rubber cape — stops at a crossroads. He shouts something, with one foot on the ground for support. Beneath the green cape he is clutching Grandma under his arm. Her urn.

The spider is an employee at the graveyard and knows where to look. He gets off his bicycle and they follow him. Dad hangs back to light a cigarette. Grandpa and Aunt Laura are unaware of it, but something alarming is going on in Lund. She can't talk to anyone about it. Definitely not Dad.

They follow the man through wet grass, past monuments and graves surrounded by iron chains, past gravestones adorned with doves and marble angels. At last they reach the family grave. It is almost invisible, a small flat stone with three family names and a hole that has been dug beneath a tree by the path. The fact that one of the family names is hers sends an uncomfortable pang through her body. She remembers the dead hare, half-eaten.

The rain drips from the branches of the trees as Dad and Laura place Grandma's remains in the hole. Grandpa's cheeks are wet with tears, or is it rain? No one says anything. The employee takes his leave and gets back on his bicycle.

The gravestone is no bigger than a briefcase.

Beneath it lies a whole collection of people. Seven or eight individuals. Laura knows who they all are. Grandma's parents. Grandma's maternal grandmother's sister. Grandma's two unmarried sisters. Grandpa and Grandma's first child, little Karin, who died before Laura was born. Just one man, Grandma's unknown father, has dragged a flock of women along with him.

And presumably the grave contains not only bones and ash, but unimaginable unknown sorrows and tears. Here lies her father's family, undemanding, unassuming, and thrifty. No airs and graces. No exaggerated pomp. No big words.

They stand in silence in the pouring rain in front of the least prepossessing gravestone in the whole churchyard; it is shockingly modest. All those unknown souls from Småland who came to Stockholm and were poor. But who battled through adversity.

Aunt Laura and Grandpa take the subway to Västertorp.

She and Dad are going to visit Ricki and Olle. What is she supposed to say to Dad? He's lost his mom. And even though she didn't really get to know Grandma herself, she realizes that Dad loved her very much, and is very upset.

And he doesn't say anything, apart from *So, that was that then,* as he cups his hand around a match, which could mean just about anything. *So.* It's over. There are no words.

And then he says they should have time to go to the liquor store, which they do, and Dad buys a bottle of Grönstedts cognac. She would have liked to say something special about Grandma, but she can't come up with anything that doesn't sound artificial. That's one of the distinguishing features of Dad's side of the family: they take pride in never saying anything pretentious. Never exaggerating. No hysteria. Dad's family is very different from Mom's.

They walk along Regeringsgatan and it is pouring, a peevish, persistent rain. Dad tucks his hand under her arm and jokes. Ricki resigned from HSB as soon as she found out she was pregnant: sanguine, overconfident, and thoughtless. It didn't work out; she and Olle soon found themselves short of money. Now she is employed at the Defense Factory Works.

The apartment on Drottninghusgränd is as warm as a greenhouse. Olle is delighted with the cognac, and gets out the glasses. There is some talk about Olle's job; he sells radios for Philips, and isn't happy. She hasn't seen Ricki for a long time. She has grown rounder; the former elegant dress sense is no more.

But being close to Ricki still feels like stroking silk, soft and exclusive. She accompanies her into the little nursery. The boy, who is two years old, is awake; he is sitting quietly on his cot.

He has a strange, slightly egg-shaped head. He doesn't make a sound. He doesn't take his eyes off Ricki, and his expression is unfathomable. Ricki picks him up and breast-feeds him; they make her think of the Italian sculpture called the *Pietà*: a mother and son. Jesus after he was taken down from the cross.

During the hours in Ricki's presence, she becomes calm.

Life is normal in Ricki's apartment, she thinks. Five strangers are sharing the sleeping car with her. She lies awake, listening as the wheels of the train jolt over the points. From then on she visits Ricki whenever she gets the chance.

• • •

She never asks Ricki about personal matters, not even when they are alone together. Olle is at work and Ricki is standing at the sink in overalls, peeling potatoes. She has tied an unflattering scrap of fabric around her soft hair.

She isn't at work because she has been feeling a little dizzy.

Nothing to worry about, Ricki says, even though knives and forks keep jumping out of her hands and falling on the floor.

Everything will sort itself out if you take what comes, she says. That's exactly what Dad sings in the shower; it's a song by Ernst Rolf. Ricki says she likes puttering around at home. When she's at work they have a child minder who looks after the boy during the day.

The two of them, Ricki and Olle, have experienced what it is like to be totally accepted by another person. She will never experience that. She finishes with one boy after another. When it is over, she grieves. Every single time she grieves as if her heart would break, even when she did the dumping.

The boy has learned to walk. With light, rapid steps he makes his way from the living room, through the kitchen, into his nursery, and back again. Over and over again. He is pale and has a slight stoop. Three years old, never says a word. There is no need; his parents love him, and words are superfluous.

Nothing abnormal, Ricki says when she asks anyway.

Boys often start talking late. Ricki has read up about it, nothing to worry about. After they have eaten, the boy fetches his Donald Duck comic, and Ricki takes him on her knee and reads to him. Huey, Dewey, and Louie are messing around as usual. The Beagle Boys are plotting something bad. Mean old Uncle Scrooge falls asleep on top of his piles of gold.

The boy follows the story with rapt attention, gazing at the pictures with that inscrutable expression. Everything is fine, apart from their finances, Ricki says, smiling at her across the kitchen table. Unfortunately they don't have enough money. And Olle comes home from work.

Their joy when they see each other again is palpable. They call the boy their precious baby and embrace with him between them.

If love does exist, it is here.

Do you believe in God? She hadn't intended to ask, but it just comes out. On this occasion: summer. They are sitting in the asphalted yard at Drottninghusgränd with a tray of coffee on a stool between them. Olle has gone for a walk with the precious baby. A vigorous ivy is climbing up the wall.

She is pretty sure that Ricki will say no. In her family no one believes in God, except maybe Aunt Laura. No one talks about him, and no one goes to church. But Ricki answers yes, actually, she does believe.

She wants to know what Ricki means. Do you believe in a kindly old man who fixes everything, with our best interests at heart?

No, Ricki replies, not an old man exactly, more like Spinoza. She doesn't really succeed in giving a detailed explanation of how she believes in God in accordance with Spinoza.

The harmony, she ventures. Someone must have worked it out. Calibrated it. Made everything miraculously fit together — the circulation of the blood, gravity, the orbits of the planets. Not an old man, more a kind of spirit.

The doves are moving around on the asphalt. The male puffs himself up, the female isn't interested, runs away. The male tires of the pursuit and pecks at crumbs until he puffs himself up once more and starts chasing a new female. What is she supposed to think about what Ricki is saying?

I believe in a world consciousness, Ricki goes on.

A world sense.

At that point she raises an objection. The world is anything but sensible, it is crazy. The Nazis' annihilation of the Jews, the murder of the Indians in America, and most recently the Suez Crisis, the British bombed Cairo and then Russian tanks rolled into Hungary and many people believe there will be a third world war.

Absolutely, Ricki interrupts her, picking a flake of pastry off her blouse and popping it in her mouth. Absolutely, people do terrible things. But I still believe there is a world consciousness, and that harmony is the basic template. Balance. You just have to follow that route and do your best.

Route? What route?

I mean love, Ricki replies. Eros is everywhere, even in the most mundane elements of our lives. In sensuality. In joy. Perhaps it is there most of all, and least of all in church. Love isn't just loving one person after another, you know. But if you love a person completely from the inside, something happens. Love becomes a force.

Eros, Ricki goes on after a while. It can be cooking a meal. Doing the ironing. Anything at all. The simplest of tasks. Eros is when body and soul come together. That is the route, or maybe I should call it the way, she says.

After a brief pause she adds that she would like to have been a Buddhist, a peaceful religion. The sun moves slowly across the courtyard.

No one has ever talked to the girl like this before. It is also the only philosophical conversation she has with her aunt Ricki. It doesn't last long. It is interrupted by Olle, who has come home and is standing at the window in his shirtsleeves, calling for them to come in. What was it Ricki said? It was so simple that it sounded naive.

What she remembers most clearly afterward is Ricki's immutable, stubborn confidence. It stuck with her, and it became a counterbalance to all the other stuff, everything that was evasive, half-spoken, embarrassed. But I didn't understand that until much later: the fact that Ricki was the only counterbalance that was given to me.

• • •

To make body and soul come together? Easier said than done. She is with one boy after another. The restlessness consumes her with hungry jaws. It forces her out virtually every night, and the door between body and soul is firmly closed. All kinds of things happen simultaneously, but in separate parts of her.

One evening Dad tests her on her Latin homework. He doesn't know any Latin, and he finds it entertaining. He is lying on the bed and she is sitting at her desk, explaining the vocative and ablative cases to him. Mom flings open the door; she is furious.

Look at you, lying there making out with your own daughter too!

The front door slams behind her. That's sick. Dad stays where he is, the Latin grammar open on his chest. It is dark outside. Mom is out there with her lame leg, her jealousy, the state of the roads, and the ditches, the inadequate street lighting, the cars, the poor visibility in the mist.

She forces Dad to go after her.

He doesn't want to. He really doesn't want to. She knows that. She sees the look in his eyes: tormented. Then acquiescent. She makes him go out and search for Mom. She remains sitting at her desk. Inside her head she can hear the reverberation of the accusations Mom has probably flung at Dad. And his responses, evasive as usual.

Matter-of-fact, but evasive. She can hear Mom's obstinacy, the hammer on the nail, *bang*. Mom's tongue is horrific, as sharp as a sword, slicing through soft tissue. At last she hears them return, and manages to get her body to obey her once more.

I was furious with Mom. I defended Dad when I spoke to her. It wasn't Dad I was defending, but myself. I didn't want to be dragged into it all.

I didn't want to. *Your own daughter. Too.* The words offended me.

They sexualized my relationship with my father. As if he would have made out with me! Your own daughter too! For a long time after this incident I pictured myself splitting open my mother's head with a spike. She fell to the ground, blood spurting everywhere. The vision would come particularly when I was trying to get to sleep: Mom's skull splintering, the blood gushing out. I wanted to stop seeing it, but it kept on coming back.

It became a compulsion inside my head, like the knife.

And in spite of the fact that I wanted it to stop, I smashed my mother's skull over and over again. It was a compulsion, but I was the one responsible for it. And this repulsiveness brought with it an unpleasant sense of satisfaction.

Everything happens simultaneously but in entirely separate parts of her. She is a member of the school drama group. They rehearse in the basement. She is the secretary of the well-established school society known as Scenia, and in that capacity she welcomes the actor Max von Sydow down in the basement.

He is accompanied by a journalist and a photographer.

He too used to attend the Cathedral School, and was secretary of the drama group. As the photographer takes pictures she plucks up the courage to ask how one becomes an actor, and he answers in a friendly way. There is a feature in *Vecko-Journalen* with his remarkable, gnarled face on the cover.

It reminds her of a cross-looking knot on the trunk of a birch tree.

In the background it is just possible to glimpse a shadow, which is her.

She is obsessed with film and theater. She sees Max von Sydow play Peer Gynt, directed by Ingmar Bergman, at the city theater in Malmö. She remembers his raging fury. She would love to have the courage to release such fury.

She remembers the Button Molder, who wanted to melt down and remold Peer's soul. And the words about how life is like an onion, its layers being peeled away to reveal that it contains nothing. Of course that's the way it is, she thinks: nothing. Even though she is still in high school, she is a member of the student film studio and the student jazz club, Klubb 52. She plays truant from school to visit the Danish Film Museum in Copenhagen with her friends.

The Cabinet of Dr.Caligari, swathed in mist and spooky smoke.

The murderers are amongst us, with the remarkable Peter Lorre and his terrified, guilt-filled eyes. Viking Eggeling's films, which consist only of abstract patterns, an ever-changing kaleidoscope, life's flickering images. Perhaps he is saying that the contours of life are constantly shifting, and this is freedom.

Standing in front of a screen or a stage, she feels free. And that is virtually the only time.

In the middle of winter she hitchhikes to Gothenburg. The roads are treacherous with ice. She has to stand there for a long time in the bitter wind, thumb in the air. She wants to ask Aunt Laura how Ricki met Olle. Is that why she goes there, and not because she's worried?

When she arrives, Aunt Laura doesn't ask how she got there; she simply offers prawn sandwiches and is as chatty as ever.

And she tells the story of how Ricki met Olle.

To put it briefly: The charter holiday Ricki booked in 1952 was miserable, and Ricki soon regretted her decision. She might just as well have stayed at home and looked after Grandma, thus avoiding her intrusive fellow travelers and tedious visits to museums. On the boat trip to Madeira, she was sharing a cabin with three very talkative ladies.

Seasickness saved her from their company. The sea was rough, the sky overcast. She leaned over the railing, unable to stop throwing up. A man she had never seen before came over and expressed his concern. She tried to get him to go away, but he refused. She waved her hand, but he took no notice.

He placed his hand on her forehead as she vomited.

Gave her water afterward. Wrapped his coat around her. Ricki was shivering and shaking, and he took care of her. Was that Olle? Yes. Aunt Laura's tone grows warm. Did she sleep with him in a cave? Laura is taken aback. Olle was on the same boat to Funchal, on his way to sell ladies' underwear.

However, they had to say goodbye to each other, because he was married. Married? She didn't know that. Yes, he was married to a woman in the Canaries. When Ricki got home from her holiday she called Laura and told her all about it. At long last she had found a man she wanted, but he was tied to someone else. Uncle Elis was dead and Laura was lonely; Ricki often went to Gothenburg to seek solace with her sister.

In blizzards and in sunshine. When she couldn't bear it anymore. She was exhausted and in despair, and Laura did her best to console her.

Ricki as Niobe, all tears.

A grieving Andromache who has lost her Hector.

She has never seen Ricki like that. She can't even imagine her calm aunt behaving that way. But she listens to Laura's story like a five-year-old entranced by a fairy tale. She needs a story with a happy ending. After a long wait, over a year, Olle wrote to say that he was free and on his way to Sweden. They got married and had their precious baby.

Laura makes up a bed for her in Uncle Elis's room.

She tosses and turns, she can't sleep. What if Olle hadn't gone up on deck that night when Ricki was seasick? What if she had chosen a different destination? What if he had stayed in the lounge with the other passengers, enjoying a few drinks?

Just one tiny detail and they would have missed each other. Was it the fortune-teller's prediction that made them meet up?

It was probably because they were both open to love. Which is just as much of a miracle as a prediction being fulfilled. Maybe predictions should be regarded as suggestions for new roads to take, different thoughts to consider. A prediction can make new aspects of life appear. At that moment, believing in miracles seems to her to be eminently sensible.

• • •

Life is a series of glissandos. Disharmonies. It is an uneasy music, but sometimes a particular note can be heard. A soft clarinet, a fragile violin.

Sometimes she can hear it. The rest of the time she is nothing more than a cycling paper doll, tossed up by the wind into the great skies that cover Lund, sunshine yellow and dizzying. There is another life, there has to be.

She and her boyfriend manage to get into a dance at the Academic Society; she starts laughing so hard she can't stop. She gets drunk on laughter. They are dancing in the big room at the Ateneum and a fantastic band is playing. Suddenly a woman — slightly older and a student — comes up to her and throws her arms around her.

Honey, I hope you always stay this happy.

She stands there on the dance floor, completely taken aback. Her arms drop to her sides and she watches the woman walk away. What an odd thing to happen. And what a lovely thing to say. It was so nice to be hugged by a strange woman, who seems to know something about life, maybe something sorrowful and bitter.

But did she think the girl was happy, just because she was laughing?

Yes, she has a boyfriend. He is in his final year at high school, he is interested in literature and introduces her to the writers of the 1940s: Sven Alfons, Karl Vennberg, and Axel Liffner, who are so modern that the school's history of literature course doesn't get as far as them (although Alf Henriques does; she buys his book on modern literature from Gleerups).

They usually hang out on his bed, reading aloud to each other. He particularly likes Ingemar Gustafsson, the author from Lund who later becomes Leckius. His novellas are improbable and make her head spin.

There's the one about the man who is born inside a nutshell, lives his life, and dies there. It captures perfectly that feeling of being shut in. A tale about being depressed.

The boy doesn't understand what she means. The radiator is humming. They soon move on to caressing each other. He teaches her a lot of useful things, like the best way to handle a penis.

She appreciates the knowledge. She likes him too. He is good and kind and gives her rides on his Vespa. But she doesn't tell him about the drama at home; sometimes it seems like a fight to the death.

There is just one occasion, when he is in her room, and they hear her parents' angry voices from the living room; she unexpectedly lets out a dry sob. She hears herself say that she thinks her parents are going to split up.

The boyfriend looks astonished. I'm just being silly, she says. She feels as if she is exaggerating, trying to make herself look important, as if she were fishing for his sympathy.

She immediately pulls herself together and dismisses what she said. Soon they are laughing over something; later she can't remember what it was.

But that relationship doesn't last either.

Maybe it's precisely because things are good between them. Because they could simply carry on like this, with no real effort. She thought that would be unbearable. Maybe he was too stable. Too reliable. Too thoughtful. Simply too good. But it was mostly because he couldn't numb her anxiety. She seeks those who are torn to pieces. Those who are broken.

She feels at home with them. In a bitter wind that excoriates her soul. As usual she grieves when it's over. No one loves her. She doesn't even love herself.

Everyone is in disguise. Everyone wears a mask. No one is honest. Including her. That's the way life works. That's why she likes the theater.

Behind the masks lies the power. It can't be seen, but it's there. It makes the teachers afraid, especially the young trainee teachers. They all know it exists, but it remains hidden while other things are discussed. Democracy. Evil in the Soviet Union. Just about anything, although nothing really hangs together.

One can see life as a series of appearances onstage.

And accept the role one is given.

Or roles; there are many, all different. She knows that. Why not accept that one is playing roles? And stop regarding oneself as a stern judge. In the spring of her third year she is given the lead in Scenia's school revue, a role she completely adores.

First of all there is the disguise itself, the costume.

She is to wear a black dress, close-fitting with a low neck. She makes it herself out of black acetate lining, which is cheap. The fabric is slinky and hard to handle and slips through her fingers as she sits at Mom's Elna. Ninne has to help her pin it when she tries it on in front of the mirror.

She takes it in a little, then a little more. She is going to wear Lund's most provocative dress. Her heels will be as high as the Empire State Building. She cycles all the way to the shoe store in Lomma, which sells remaindered factory stock, and her heels are so high that she can hardly walk in them.

She is going to wear a black top hat. She wants to be able to toss her hair over her shoulders. She aims to look like Juliette Gréco, who sings Boris Vian and Jacques Prévert in the nightclubs of Paris. She hasn't heard her sing, but she has seen photographs of her. She will be just like Gréco. French, alluring, depraved.

With black eyebrows, zinc-white lips and a *mouche* on her cheek.

They rehearse in the basement, then as the performance grows closer they move into the music room, which is in an annex in the schoolyard and has a stage. The revue is being written by a group of fourth-year students — daring dialogues about the teachers, provocative lyrics set to well-known jazz tunes. She practices her numbers with the band, which is made up of her school friends.

A piano. A bass. A drum set. A saxophonist who also plays the clarinet. The boys are going to wear T-shirts with horizontal stripes and top hats. They are very kind and transpose the music for her to hide the deficiencies in her voice.

She's no singer. Mom made that clear to her right from the get-go. She has eaten chalk to try to make her voice deeper and avoid the choral singing.

But if you don't believe in yourself, you're no one. Better to behave as if you did. Put your trust in God or the Devil. Believe in miracles. She decides that is exactly what she is going to do. She is going to sing, bellow, roar.

The main thing is to be magnificent. And dramatic. She has a kind of talent for the latter, and that is the role she is to play. Seductress, femme fatale. Temptress. Slut and siren. She feels honest in this role. All roles contain elements of the truth.

Not the whole truth, but elements of it. No roles are wrong if you are honest. And who said you can't choose your own? During rehearsals she becomes a different person. It is overwhelming. She is also desperate to be seen. The tall beech tree in the schoolyard is just coming into leaf, but the evenings are mercilessly cold. They practice clambering up a tall, rickety ladder from the yard to the music room on the second floor.

The audience will use the normal entrance and the staircase. Dizziness, butterflies in her tummy. Everybody shivers at the foot of the ladder, but they are warmed by their nerves, stage fright, and anticipation.

The premiere is packed. So many people turn up that some have to stand at the back, behind the rows of chairs. Whenever she is about to appear she has to climb that rickety ladder in her high heels, which means she has to pull her tight dress right up over her thighs.

The janitor, who is holding the ladder, smacks her on the bottom and makes inappropriate comments of a sexual nature on every single occasion. She doesn't have time to worry about that. She just hopes he steadies the ladder properly; she doesn't want to fall and break her leg before she has managed to win over her audience.

•   •   •

And win them over she does. The music room is full to bursting with students from her school, students from other schools, parents, curious teachers, and hopefully one or two journalists.

She steps into the spotlight. Her cheeks are burning, there is a rushing sound in her ears. The tension is unbearable as the band strikes up.

With a flamboyant gesture she removes the top hat. Her best number is the irreverent, sensual lullaby toward the end; it's about the flirtatious Geography teacher, and is set to the music from the film *Rififi* by the director Jules Dassin. She copies the teacher's mannerisms as she pushes her hair off her forehead; lots of people recognize him, and start to applaud.

First he's strict and then he smiles,
Asks those cheeky questions,
That's his Ri fi fi . . .

The audience is virtually ecstatic. And she sucks on the notes and wiggles her hips, she roars and throws one leg forward, kicks out with her foot. They love her and her ironic exaggerations. They whistle and stamp their feet and clap their hands.

She is a woman. That is the role she is playing.

Slut, seductress, subjugator: that is her role, and she revels in the power it gives her. As she takes her bow she feels dizzy with happiness. She wants to be exactly like the character she is playing.

And that is what she intends to do.

The revue is a *succès formidable*. Many people say so, including the director who has actually been to the nightclubs of Paris. Her contribution to its success was far from insignificant. During recess she stands outside the tobacconist's opposite the school, where they sell loose Bill, and reads about herself in the newspaper. Third professor's daughter to appear in a revue in Lund.

Following in the footsteps of Yvonne Lombard and Cilla Ingvar.

With a big photograph of her in the dress and the top hat, with the *mouche* on her cheek. The picture isn't unflattering. Her cheeks are a little too full, her eyes a fraction too childish. And perhaps she is slightly too chubby for the dress, which is creased over her stomach. But no, she looks good.

Practically smashing, in fact.

She realizes that she could be exactly that. She stuffs the paper into her coat pocket and runs across the street in the naked light of spring to get to her lesson in time. She admires her Latin teacher; he is a poet, and she reads his anthologies with genuine appreciation. He has a particular way of handing back their exercise books when he has marked them: he tosses them through the air in an elegant arc, so that each one lands unerringly on the right desk.

Of course some people prefer to strut around on a stage. The Latin teacher's tone is sarcastic. There is no possibility of misunderstanding his words; he is talking about her. She didn't have much time to prepare for the test, and no doubt she has paid the price.

Quickly and nervously she flicks through until she finds her grade.

A-minus. So what is he talking about?

It is true that she struts around on a stage. But for the time being she decides to take the comment as a kind of back-handed recognition. She has just turned seventeen. She is a woman and she is smashing.

The final performance, the last time in the spotlight. She is feeling more and more at ease. She tosses her hair over her shoulder and brings out the seductive Rififi. She is in the middle of the number and her eyes have gotten used to the bright light when she catches sight of him. Dad is at the back of the room. With Vibeke.

She is holding her little boy in her arms.

They are standing close together.

Seeing them gives her a bit of a shock, but she finishes the number. She takes off her hat and bows to the audience, glancing in their direction. They have gone. They must have come in toward the end of the show. And slunk out again.

During the wild, high-spirited party at her classmate Eva's apartment after the final performance, she realizes she can no longer ignore *the way things are.*

She gets drunk. She chatters and kisses everyone and everyone tells her how brilliant it was and babbles away. She totters out onto the balcony with a glass of wine in one hand and a cigarette in the other. The night air, with its sharp edge of spring chill, sobers her up. She has to look reality in the eye.

Mom is in the psychiatric clinic in Lund.

That's the way things are. While she has been rehearsing and strutting around onstage, Mom hasn't been at home. She hasn't asked why, she has only thought about being allowed to show off in the school revue. Many people see her as tough and self-confident. Which means she has been able to fool both them and herself. She stands on the balcony at Eva's and looks up at the stars. The light has traveled for millions of years to reach her eyes.

This time the stars provide no solace. What are they doing to Mom in the psychiatric clinic, why is she there? Anxiety, a faithful companion throughout her life, reports for duty.

The following day she stays home from school. She doesn't get up until late morning; she pulls on some clothes and opens her books. But at lunchtime Dad turns up. With Vibeke and the boy.

No doubt he didn't expect to find anyone in the apartment.

They are perfectly pleasant. They don't mention the revue, but they ask her to look after the boy; they have something important to discuss. The boy is very cute. They lie on their tummies on the floor in her room and she draws cartoons telling stories about everything he asks for: giraffes, monsters, cars. The important discussion takes a long time.

The boy starts to get anxious, wanting his mommy. Should she stop him from going to look for her? She opens the door and he rushes out. She deliberately follows him. Vibeke is lying on the couch in the living room. Dad is half-lying on top of her, caressing her. Vibeke's skirt is pushed right up and her thighs are visible.

She immediately goes back to her room.

Now she knows for sure. She can no longer turn a blind eye.

After a while they call out to her from the kitchen. They've made coffee, would she like some? They look perfectly normal.

All their buttons are done up. Vibeke is sitting with the little boy on her knee, her smile just as warm and untroubled as always. Vibeke knows that she saw them, of course. Dad must also realize that she is aware of the situation.

But they act as if nothing has happened. By doing so they make a demand of her: that she must do the same.

To know and to give nothing away is to be split in two. Her head and her heart are torn. What is infidelity? It is having a sexual relationship with another man's wife. Does Uncle Bertil know that his wife is having sex with his close friend? Does he accept the situation? And Mom, what does she know?

She hopes she has got it wrong. She tries to convince herself that's what's happened. They like one another, of course they do. They just make out a little. They think it's cool.

But she hasn't got it wrong. Objectively she recalls one incident after another over the past few years. They are having a relationship, and presumably it has been going on for a long time. Vibeke, who turned up with the boy at the house in the archipelago last summer. They stood in the kitchen with the boy and hugged each other.

And Mom didn't come down; she stayed upstairs. The girl went up to her after a while. She was lying in bed, smoking. The girl asked her to come down, but Mom shook her head. She tried to take the brandy bottle away from her, and Mom rapped her sharply across the knuckles. *Go away!*

Everything falls into place. At the same time nothing makes sense. Vibeke, who said to her afterward, when Mom didn't come down: I feel sorry for you, having a mom who's so sick. How *dare* Vibeke say such a thing! How did she have the gall to turn up at all? To join them on Kullen? To appear with Mom in the *St. John Passion*?

Could they have been together for that long? What if Vibeke's little boy is Dad's too — is that why he stayed away in America when the child was born? No, that's unthinkable. How can Dad seem so blasé about the whole thing? Or is he just not facing up to the situation?

Perhaps he's burying his head in the sand, like an ostrich.

And Vibeke is doing the same. If you don't admit it, it doesn't exist. Is that what's going on? She turns it over and over in her mind. Dismisses her thoughts. Forces herself to think them again. Maybe Bertil does know. Maybe he thinks it's okay. Maybe that's how he and Dad cement their warm friendship, by loving the same woman.

A crazy idea. Totally perverted.

Maybe Dad is drawn to warm, cheerful Vibeke as a motherly figure? He misses Grandma, and Mom is neither cheerful nor particularly motherly. Or maybe Vibeke went after him, and Dad — who is always so reluctant to hurt anyone — couldn't end it. Once they'd started.

So many possibilities. There's no point in trying to work out how they feel or the reality of the situation. She still won't be able to understand. The only thing she knows for sure is that it could be one way or another.

They're having a relationship. Or they're not having a relationship.

From a logical point of view, one excludes the other.

It is very difficult to accommodate two such contradictory truths. So how is she supposed to deal with this?

It turns inward. Either she has to trust the evidence of her senses and her intellect, which means she is a co-conspirator with Dad and Vibeke.

And it means she is culpable too, in a way.

Or she keeps on telling herself that it's all a figment of her imagination. In which case she becomes blurred and unclear. If she is going to be able to understand who she is, and to be honest, then she has to trust what her eyes and her intellect are telling her, and not allow herself to become a vague smudge. She would love to behave like Dad, and bury her head in the sand. Refuse to engage with the matter. If they are together, then so what? Nothing to do with her.

But she can't behave like an ostrich.

How can Dad have been so calm, so cheerful over the years if he's been leading a double life? And Mom, constantly fishing for the truth, running after it so to speak, while being betrayed.

Why is Mom really in the psychiatric clinic? Does she know? And should the girl choose to *realize* or continue to *look away*? It's an important choice. Practically a philosophical choice. She wants to be able to see clearly. She wants to be true. But how can she be true if everything around her is a lie? The more pressing question is how she is going to deal with her parents. To put it simply: *how is she going to behave toward them?*

• • •

Dad brings Mom home from the clinic in the old Hanomag. They didn't get a new car after all. He has bought pork chops and fries them for dinner.

He opens a bottle of wine to celebrate her return.

They sit around the kitchen table, the whole family. She gazes at her mother's long fingers as they pick a match out of the box with a movement that is so familiar, and light a cigarette. A pianist's fingers, as Dad used to say.

She can't talk to them. She doesn't even try. Which of them would she turn to? During the period that follows, something I referred to as the *terror of silence* became a reality. You have to watch what you say. Make sure you don't come out with the wrong thing. Keep quiet about what she isn't sure if Mom knows, the knowledge that could lead to disaster.

Disaster? Really? But many people are involved: her parents, Bertil and Vibeke, and their children. She has no way of knowing who knows what. Maybe the whole town knows? Apart from Mom, possibly.

But obviously Mom knows everything, she thinks.

Which means that Mom must have exercised a heroic level of self-control, which occasionally faltered. And who can blame her?

At regular intervals she once again tries to tell herself that it's *just her imagination.* That she dreamed up Vibeke on the couch underneath Dad. But she didn't. She gets stuck in the fissure between truth and lies.

Surely something must happen? Nothing happens. Catharsis is the high point in classical drama, when the reality becomes clear and the audience is faced with the truth. This is a drama with no catharsis. She knows what she saw.

And she doesn't trust either of them. If her parents' life is a play, she thinks it's dreadful. She concludes that she and her sisters have grown up in a lie. Nothing has been as it appeared to be. That hurts.

And keeping quiet hurts most of all.

The photographs from that period. One of Ninne's confirmation. Oh yes, after me Ninne was confirmed too. In this picture: Mom at the piano, calm and collected, hands hovering over the keys, an almost ecstatic smile on her face. Dad, without a care in the world, one arm around Ninne in her white dress. Ia, half-grown, in a checked dress with a cross around her neck. And me, relaxed and smiling next to Ia, in a woolen dress with a broad patent belt. I remember the dress was itchy. Everything else has been erased. A forgotten photographer said *cheese* and we all smiled.

A snapshot of a very happy family.

But the way I remember it: my last year in school was nothing more than a protracted wait for school to be over. I stopped smoking and didn't care if I got fat.

I was living in Lund, a delightful academic town. The mendacity was hidden well, but not entirely. Certain authors in Lund wrote about it. Fritjof Nilsson Piraten (*Three Semesters*). Hjalmar Gullberg (*Love in the Twentieth Century*). Bold, sharp Majken Johansson with her careless irony. I read Anna Rydstedt's poems and heard her recite them at the Academic Society.

I eat next to nothing these days, a little bread, a few crumbs from the happiness of others. Something along those lines. The poems reached me, but through a thick mist. And reality was cloven in two like a tree struck by lightning.

Shortly before she graduates from high school she is home alone with Mom. She thinks it over, then asks why she was in the clinic. Because I suffer from depression, Mom says.

And why is that? Mom says it's always been that way. They are sitting in the living room. The potted plants in the window are barely breathing, and the twilight is no more than a shimmer of yellow. And Mom tells her about Jetty, a little girl who became her playmate when she acquired a baby brother. He was sick, and Granny had to spend a lot of time with him. Mom got Jetty instead.

And they played together all day. She was four years old, and strictly forbidden from going out through the iron gate in Surabaja on her own. One day Jetty, who was full of ideas, thought it would be good if they went for a walk. The servants were otherwise occupied, and the gate was open. Clutching each other's hands they headed for the Red Bridge among the crowds of pedestrians, street traders, and ox carts.

Suddenly Granddad loomed up before them like an enraged bull elephant. He dragged her home. When she refused to admit that she had been disobedient, he locked her in his big closet. She stood there for hours, kicking and screaming.

When the key turned it was night. Once again he demanded that she admit she had gone out through the gate alone. She refused. She hadn't been alone. Jetty was with her. He locked her in again.

She screamed until her voice gave out. When Granddad finally opened the door for the second time, he demanded that she admit that Jetty didn't exist. She refused, and was beaten. After all those hours in the closet, she was no longer able to speak. She developed nodules on her vocal chords and couldn't make a sound. For over a year.

Of course Jetty didn't exist, Mom says.

But she seemed so alive that Mom didn't realize. She told the truth, but still got beaten. Since then she has suffered regular episodes of depression. Mom says she believes she has always had another world, a fantasy world, within her. She had never been able to share it with others; instead, music took up all the space available.

And she wasn't good enough. The nerves. The anxiety. The sense of inadequacy. No, she wasn't good enough for the music. Mom sounds sad, but she's calm. She hopes Mom will mention Vibeke, that it will be possible to discuss the whole thing openly. But Mom doesn't mention Vibeke.

Which means she dare not mention her either.

Mom says that she asked to be admitted to the clinic. She wanted to understand her anxiety, her depression, once and for all. But the professor wasn't interested in what she had to say. He interrupted her and declared that her depression was endogenous. Which means hereditary.

She was given electric shock treatment to counteract her endogenous depression. They secured her to the bed with straps and sent electric currents through her head. This was repeated several times. The patient shakes, the limbs jerk uncontrollably. She flaps around like a fish out of water and the nurse stuffs a rag into her mouth.

It's a bit like epilepsy, Mom says.

It sounds like torture, the girl thinks.

But the electric shocks didn't help. When she told the professor she was just as depressed afterward and that she wanted to go home, he replied that she ought to undergo a *sleep cure*.

That was the only thing that could fix her.

But Mom had seen the somnambulists around the clinic, drugged to the eyeballs, tottering along like zombies, not entirely asleep but robbed of their mind. She couldn't agree to that.

You're not touching my mind!

She slammed her hand down on the desk. When the professor insisted, she got frightened. She ran away from the clinic and called Dad from a telephone kiosk. She sat on her suitcase in a snow-covered field smoking cigarettes until he came and picked her up.

I feel sorry for your dad, she says, having to put up with a depressive like me. But at least I know now, she adds, that I am suffering from an endogenous depression, and that it's incurable.

They are sitting opposite one another at the coffee table and forget to switch on the lights. Outside darkness is falling.

Mom has been honest. The girl would like to continue the conversation. Surely depression can't be incurable? Something must have caused it.

But the moment has passed. Dad arrives home with Ninne and Ia, and there is no opportunity to bring up the matter again.

Afterward she is shaken. She knows who the professor of psychiatry is. He is the father of one of her classmates. He is a kindly, absentminded gentleman who seems to be from another planet, but he didn't want to talk to her mother. Didn't want to listen to what she had to say about her life.

And of course if he had listened, Mom might have accused her husband of having triggered her depression through his infidelity. A colleague! The professors of Lund are above that kind of tittle-tattle. No doubt they stick together, form a scientific front against their wives. Being unfaithful is probably regarded as perfectly natural, nothing to worry about. If a woman is betrayed and reacts with rage and despair, science explains that she is suffering from endogenous depression.

But Mom hasn't said anything about Vibeke, even though she announced not very long ago that Vibeke couldn't be trusted. And after Mom comes home from the clinic, she and Dad are very nice to each other. The whole thing is beyond her comprehension.

She lives in a state of uncertainty, like the interface between night and day, when contours are erased. When you hear a scream and you don't know where it's coming from — a perfectly ordinary bird or a mask with an evil grin. You know and you don't know.

It is possible to exist in that state for quite a long time. You are enveloped in a lack of clarity which is unpleasant, but also merciful. It makes life bearable. At least it's not too bad, existing in this state of incompatible truths.

They say that truth is indivisible. But in fact it is incomplete, because it has nasty sharp edges.

•   •   •

He serves tea, fragrant tea in a pretty little cup. He sits down opposite her, his legs tucked beneath him on the sofa. His black hair is shining. The room is light and airy, with colorful oil paintings on the walls.

She contemplates his young yet slightly aged face. The tea-cups are on the table between them. His face — no, not aged, merely inexpressibly wise.

She trusts him. Everything is drifting, just a little.

The weeks before graduation from high school are endless. She often goes to the movies, and tonight, cycling home: a flat tire. Disaster. Mårtenstorget is deserted, apart from two cops ambling across the cobblestones. No point in asking them for help. Particularly as the light on her bicycle has also given up the ghost.

Everything is falling apart. Pushing the bicycle all the way home is too much for her; she has no strength left. Suddenly the man is standing by her side.

Short. Immensely polite. Japanese, it turns out. Unfortunately he can't do anything about the flat tire, but may he offer her a cup of tea? She feels as if she is in the middle of a movie, she can't describe it any other way. That's fine. She is very happy to step out of reality and into this film. He leads her across a black backyard. Film noir, like *Le Quai des Brumes*.

Flickering lights, tall shadows in the stairwell.

Film clip. She steps into a well-lit apartment, the paintings on the walls are modern and abstract and the film switches to color. All the time, that slight drift. They exchange a few words. Not too many. Light sentences, weightless like everything else. His English is soft, gentle, his questions discreet.

So what is she intending to do after her exams?

Oh God. After she graduates from high school? Leave home. As soon as possible. She doesn't say that. I'm thinking of devoting myself to art, she says.

She is a little surprised at her boldness.

She wants to make movies. However you go about something like that, she says when he seems to be waiting for a response. No, she doesn't want to be a movie star. She shakes her head. But often she sees completely unknown people in her mind's eye, including a woman dressed in black, calling into the wind, looking a bit like Monica Vitti.

Yes? the Japanese man says encouragingly.

She goes on to say that she would like to make movies where her inner characters can be woven into the narrative, so that she can understand what they want from her. She has read about a film school in a Polish town called Lodz. She wants to study there. She doesn't think there's much chance of that, but since he's asking... That's what she would really like to do when she graduates, she explains.

The man listens. He doesn't seem to think she's being ridiculous. He nods. The room shivers, as if it were in a dream sequence. As in Michelangelo Antonioni's films, where the images are so realistic that they resemble a dream. She doesn't understand why she feels able to confide in this man, a stranger.

But the peace in this light room is restful. She has nothing more to say.

And at that point the man asks an unexpected question.

If you could choose your life, he says. If you could choose between a life that is all mapped out, with everything running smoothly, where no major disasters occur and nothing unexpected happens. And a different life with highs and lows, a life that brings despair and devastation, but also dizzying highs, ecstasy, truth, and moments of great clarity — which life would you choose?

No one has ever asked her a question like that. She has to respond. And her answer must be totally honest. It is like a prediction, but now she is the clairvoyant. She thinks about it for a long time. This is about her life.

The spheres in the paintings turn into burning balls of fire. The violet, schizophrenic lines are coasts and shipping lanes. The paintings lead her out, away from here.

She replies that she would choose a life of despair if that is the way to clarity, ecstasy, and truth. As soon as she has spoken, she knows she is being honest.

The Japanese man nods again. He would make the same choice.

And a feeling of happiness creeps in. He accompanies her back down to the street and bows to her as they stand by her bicycle. I wish you luck, he says, you will make it. And she pushes her old bicycle all the way home without even thinking about how far it is. Happiness?

That's not the right word. She no longer feels splintered.

Whole. It gives her a spurt of life. She never sees the Japanese man again. Afterward she isn't even sure where the movie began, outside which door. Maybe she was dreaming. But she chose the unforeseen, the unpredictable.

Devastation, perhaps, but also high points of great clarity. She knows her choice was true. It is one of the rare occasions when this is the case.

The day before her final exam she gives blood at the hospital in Lund; she needs the money. For once she feels so light-headed afterward that she has to prop her bicycle against a lamppost, sit down on the curb, and put her head between her knees.

Then she looks up. Strong wind.

Ragged clouds, scudding across the sky.

She has refused to buy a special dress for the end of the semester. Her confirmation dress, which Ninne also wore for her confirmation, will do perfectly well. It is raining in the morning, and she chooses her ugliest shoes — cheap, made of grayish plastic.

She just wants the whole thing to be over.

Three external examiners dressed in dark clothing are waiting in the classroom. She couldn't care less. Like most of her classmates she is given a pass and is allowed to place the student cap on her head. She stands on the steps with everyone else, gazing out across the sea of families and well-wishers in the schoolyard. Dad isn't there. He works as an external examiner in other towns. Mom isn't there either, she's involved in preparations for the party.

However, she unexpectedly spots Granny and Granddad.

Have they come all the way to Lund for her sake? They look as if they belong in a different century. Little, dark-skinned

Granny in her full-length coat and a hat with a veil. Tall, well-built Granddad in a suit, something she has never seen him wear. She is on the verge of tears. They really could have saved themselves the trouble.

So many garlands are draped around her neck that she can barely hold up her head. She is transported home in a wooden cart, pulled by some of Ninne's classmates.

OUR PRIMA DONNA, it says on a piece of cardboard.

Three boys walk in front of the cart, blowing trumpets. Progress is nerve-shatteringly slow. Angry squalls of vicious rain. This journey home is lonely and desolate. She must show gratitude. For the fact that they are there. For the flowers. The music.

She doesn't want to. She is playing a role, but in contrast to the role of prima donna, this one has been forced upon her. She stood on the stage because she wanted to be there. Now she feels as if she is stuck fast in a pot of glue. Like everyone else around her. They are stuck fast in an empty ritual, and no one can break free.

Back home Mom has made hundreds of sandwiches and there are lots of people, most around her own age. She hardly knows some of them. She doesn't want to be the reason for all this fuss, but she is. She is given a small white radio by Granny and Granddad, who are staying at the Grand Hotel. Granny pushes her lips forward in a little pout, which means they are proud of her. Proud? There's nothing to be proud of.

She plays her role. She hugs her grandparents and thanks them effusively for the radio. The punchbowl empties and the sandwiches disappear. She knows that Mom is just as unhappy as she is. Jazz and rock music boom from the phono-graph, and all those high heels are ruining Mom's newly pol-ished parquet floor.

She is the reason for all of this. And she has to look happy, just as Mom, who organized everything, has to look happy. This is the communicating vessel. The game. The mendacity. No one can be honest, or else the entire structure will collapse.

So she dances. She laughs and says thank you. She accom-panies her grandparents down to the cab, waiting outside. They get in, the cab turns the corner into Tellusgatan and is gone. The rain is taking a break.

Above the roof of the apartment block next door she sees the flashing lights of a plane on its way to Kastrup. And she cycles into town.

They move through the streets like swarms of grasshoppers. They call in at one student party after another. Laughing and singing. She does her best to get drunk, but a nail of sobriety has been hammered through her body.

School is over. Now she is faced with a black tunnel. She must enter it, and it grows narrower. She crawls along on her knees, hoping to see a light that will show there is an end to the tunnel. Then once again eyes, bodies, mouths.

As dawn breaks she wanders along beneath trees and streetlamps.

Someone is walking beside her. She knows him. She slips her arm around his waist and looks up at the lamps, which are crowned with halos of light. The gaps between the leafy branches of the trees shift and change. She and her friend climb over the fence into the Botanic Gardens.

The lilac is in bloom. The dawn chorus is striking up. His mouth is deep. His tongue tastes salty. Whatever is on the other side of graduation is shapeless.

I'm scared of the future, she says. He laughs at her, what is there to be scared of? He's intending to apply to Chalmers in Gothenburg.

After his compulsory military service — she should be glad she doesn't have that to contend with.

I'm going to Paris, she informs him. He pulls her close, still laughing. She slides her hand under his jacket and feels the warmth of his back. The sun rises higher, and the tops of the trees look as if they are on fire.

He gives her a ride home on his bicycle. She sits on the parcel shelf with her head resting on his back, feeling the movement of his muscles as he pedals along. The birds, they're singing like crazy now. From the sky: light pouring down.

There isn't a sound at home. In the kitchen she finds piles of plates waiting to be washed. Another day. Tomorrow. The bath is full; Mom has put all the flowers in there. They're dying. She feels terribly sad for them.

The flowers are dying, and all for nothing. She fishes out a few of the cards floating among the bouquets and places them on the laundry basket to dry. She opens the door of her room. Dad is on a mattress on the floor. He's home. He's pulled her quilt over him.

He's asleep. He has no pillow. He is lying on his side.

He is snoring softly. Why is he there? She doesn't have the energy to think about it. She crawls into bed and gazes down at him. His hand is resting on his cheek, the palm half-open; it looks like a child's. The daylight chisels out the lines on his face. She doesn't want to wake him. She curls up, supporting her chin on her fist, gazing down at him. She is suffused with love.

She loves him. Utterly. She is filled to the very brim with love.

To the tip of every single finger. She falls asleep in the midst of her immeasurable love for her father. When she wakes, he is gone. It turns out this was his last night at home. He has left them, and he doesn't come back.

4

an unfinished epilogue

Write.

I can't.

No one can.

It has to be said: we can't.

And yet we write.

•   •   •

It is winter. I took the car and drove here. The house is freezing. No ice covering the Sound, just assiduous efforts on the part of the water to solidify. And meanwhile: a faint jangling, tinkling, like crystal.

Pitch dark outside by three o'clock in the afternoon.

I open the front door and the darkness faces me like a wall. No lights. Not a sound, just that tinkling in the background, and the almost inaudible moaning from trees I can't see. It's not easy to write about this. So why am I trying? I take my flashlight and march over to the woodshed in my boots.

Then I get the food and whiskey out of the car. Some people say they prefer to drink in company, but for me the opposite is true. I would rather drink my whiskey alone. I started writing this a long time ago. Gather some memories, I thought at the time. Gain some clarity. They are dead. These days I usually think of them with affection. It's as if we have become the same age over the years.

Writing is challenging. It is also difficult to give up. See for yourself — look in your family albums. There are secrets preserved from one generation to the next.

And lies that help the descendants to feel proud.

But I don't want to lie. I stoke up the fire until the tiled stove is red hot. It's too cold to use the upper floor. I sit beneath the old lamp with the green beaded shade. All I can see outside is the light from the neighbor's greenhouse on Blidö.

I'll give it another try. One last try. Dad had left us.

It was only to be expected, I guess. But it was unexpected. No one had expected it. It was expected and unexpected. Mom plunges headlong, with no safety rail to save her. The three sisters are confronted by their mother's bottomless grief and rage.

Mom spends hours on the phone, they don't know who she's talking to. Dad isn't worth a candle. Nor is Vibeke. There are no words in any language to describe Vibeke's perfidy. But she is a side issue.

This is about Dad's betrayal. Mom paces around the apartment, shouting out horrible things about him. She screams and bangs her fists on the walls; they don't answer. She sits on the bed and contemplates her grazed knuckles: drops of coagulating blood. There is a hole inside her. Those injured hands cannot match the extent of the hole. She relives her life in a retrospective.

It passes before her in jerky sequences. The music she abandoned. Everything she set aside in order to support him. She bore him three children, moved house, ran the household. Mom plunges right back to the beginning of her marriage.

Was he deceiving her from the start? Has he always hidden his true feelings beneath that charming, courteous veneer? Were his daughters born against his will? Has their entire marriage been a long drawn-out sham?

In spite of everything, Mom believed they belonged together. She trusted that feeling, and him; most of the time she thought they were rock solid. That's why she often allowed herself to show her impatience, her discontent, her sense of failure.

She did it so that she could reach him behind that closed facade! As the girl listens, her parents' marriage unravels like a badly knitted sweater. It seems to have been as lacking in content as Peer Gynt's onion.

Ninne and Ia have several weeks left until the summer vacation. She is home alone with Mom. She was intending to head off to Paris after graduation. Soon she will start work at the Grand Hotel to make some money. It is as if she is standing with one foot in the air, as if she has stopped midway through a step.

She hears more than she wants to.

As she listens Dad is turned into a pathetic worm, a bootlicker, and a common liar. A flunky fawning around Mom. He went along with her wishes out of fear and to make life easier, which led to a deeper and deeper tangle of lies. Mom tried to talk to him. Pleaded with him to be honest with her.

He never responded. Not even when she produces the hotel bill that she found in his jacket when she took it to be dry-cleaned. That was before he went to America. A double room in Copenhagen. She puts the bill on the table in front of him.

Tell me the truth. Let's try and sort this out.

But he turns his face away, stares out the window, then he gets up and leaves. He doesn't even answer her! Mom thinks she is going mad. She doesn't even consider that it might be Vibeke. They are just about to start rehearsing for the *St. John Passion*. They all accompany him to the airport together when he flies to America.

During the years that follow, Mom realizes that something is wrong, although she has no idea how serious it is. One day, quite recently, she is told the truth. A friend in her musical circle draws her aside after a dinner.

You know, of course, he says. Everyone knows. Everyone also knows what Vibeke is like, she's had lots of lovers, your husband isn't the first. And everyone is on your side, her friend goes on; he suggests that someone should have a word with Dad in order to bring him to his senses.

The expression on Mom's face horrifies her friend. She obviously didn't know — what has he done?

Shocked at the knowledge that people are gossiping behind her back, Mom yells at Dad, tells him to go to hell. And he leaves. Even then he refuses to admit that it was Vibeke.

As she listens, the floor shakes. Evidently it is possible to live within a long marriage without the slightest vestige of honesty. Dad managed it.

Mom is not an enigma. But he is.

Her head is spinning. Vibeke, that's not exactly news. But how could Dad *bear* to spend all those years in silence, keeping quiet? She doesn't understand. She doesn't even want to understand. She refuses to believe that Dad is a common liar.

Perhaps it's his honorable feelings — toward Vibeke — that made him keep quiet. His *honorable feelings*? And what about those same feelings toward Mom? If Mom hadn't yelled at him, told him to go to hell, he probably wouldn't have gone.

And everything would have continued as before. But he left.

Perhaps that was what he wanted, deep down inside, so he took the opportunity. Will he come back? No one knows. *No one knows anything.* Mom broods over something he flung at her before he disappeared: You're a mollusk, I'm sick of being your nursemaid. Mom is the first to admit that she hasn't always been the way she should have been.

But mollusk, nursemaid — is that really how he has regarded their marriage? She has worked through several years when they have lived on the surface of their marriage.

And she can't abide superficiality! As she listens she has to agree; her mother is anything but superficial.

Is this what I deserve? Mom yells.

Does any woman deserve to be treated like I've been treated, by a man who is trapped within himself like an unripe fruit in its skin? *He's such a goddamn coward!* Mom screams, slamming her fist into the wall.

Then she lies down and refuses to get up. She curls up like a fetus, her back shaking. The girl doesn't know what to do. Outside it's broad daylight. The blinds are pulled right down. Mom's expression is vacant. Her skin is burning, as if she has a fever.

She mumbles, but it's impossible to make out what she is saying.

And those eyes . . . blind, empty, unfathomably deep.

No solace can be offered. And when Mom does get out of bed, she starts pacing around the apartment once again, and now she is implacable. Dad is a coward, he is not a man, not even in bed. He has trampled the most sacred things of all beneath his feet, the truthfulness of the soul, the purity and authenticity of the mind.

He has also trampled all over his daughters. His weakness is boundless. He is a pathetic little human being. He deserves the contempt of the whole world.

So this is love stripped bare. Sexuality. Eroticism. This is the god Eros, of whom Ricki spoke so beautifully. And Eros turns out to be evil. Destructive.

What she is witnessing is an amputation. A limb being torn off, the body part that is Dad's lengthy presence in Mom's life. She can only guess at how agonizingly painful it must be. She knows too little about the labyrinths of love, about the difficult interplay between honesty and lies in a marriage. About the instability of feelings and the fact that they can change.

What she sees is the appalling pain of the person who has been abandoned, in its first, uncensored version. There is no hint of expiation.

The pain is raw, like a lump of meat.

•   •   •

Over the years Dad has been a safeguard. She often thinks that without him they would be living in a madhouse. She loves him. A lot of the things Mom spits out are petty, humiliating, and untrue.

He's not an *evil* man, in spite of everything.

He's not a villain with no conscience. A little helpless in the face of the onslaught from Mom, perhaps. Maybe he didn't want to leave her, but didn't feel he could abandon Vibeke either. Of course he's done the wrong thing, there's no disputing that. But why did he do it? She is finding it difficult to think clearly.

She can't simply accept Mom's absolute condemnation. She ends up in the middle of something she finds really hard; she tries to be fair. There is no such thing as fairness in love, but she doesn't know that yet.

She tries a couple of times, just tentatively, to protest against the torrent of merciless condemnation. She is very careful. Possibly a little meddlesome. She is very frightened. She swallows hard and takes her time choosing her words. She does it to create a sense of balance so that she will be able to stand up straight.

So that the floor will not give way during this heartrending war.

But when she says, *Let's be a bit more sensible about this, I mean he's not all bad,* something happens that she can't cope with at all. Mom's fury is directed at her instead. She is informed that she is just like him. Just as weak and cowardly. A traitor, just like him. You're just like him, Mom yells.

You don't stand up for anything either. You go along with whoever is the strongest. You're scared, and you lack character — just like him! At that moment she feels she is losing her footing and falling. More than that, she feels as if she is being cast down into hell. An exaggeration, of course. But this sense of falling, plummeting, being cast down is so horrific that she stops trying to say anything positive about her father.

That's what it's like to be rejected by Mom. And since it's true — she is very scared — she doesn't do it again. A membrane of cold indifference is drawn around her so that nothing can reach her from the outside — not her friends' parties, the birds, the lush greenery and scents of spring.

She bumps into Nanna and her poodle outside the store. Nanna is bubbling over with happiness after graduating. She talks about how lovely the spring is, wanting the girl to concur. It doesn't happen. However, Nanna suggests she come around later. That sounds like a good idea; the briefest time away from home is a liberation.

She rings the bell and Nanna opens the door, delighted to see her. Welcome, come on in! She lives with her mother in a two-room apartment that is filled from floor to ceiling with books. At long last they start talking to each other. Nanna's future seems to be crystal clear, with no shadows.

She already knows that she is going to do a doctorate in the history of religion. Her thesis will look at religious perceptions in the works of Homer, so she will have to read Greek. But first she is going to study theoretical philosophy to give her *a base to build on*, as she puts it. She also writes poems, and is intending to publish them and continue writing alongside her academic career.

Which isn't at all surprising.

Nor is the fact that Nanna was reading Nietzsche in the first year at high school. She has no intention of bringing up that embarrassing encounter over her confirmation class. Nanna has probably forgotten all about it.

She becomes friends with Nanna. Who stands barefoot in her kitchen in a light summer dress making tea (Earl Grey, Lapsang Souchong, Darjeeling, Gunpowder, who knew there were all those different kinds of tea). They drink it on the balcony in white cups that have developed a patina with frequent use.

The sun is shining. Nanna rests her bare feet on the railing and talks about Lars Forssell, Gunnar Ekelöf, D. H. Lawrence, and eroticism.

The spring is spread indolently before them. And she is sitting next to Nanna, who turns out to have a detailed knowledge of eroticism, not least through female relatives who have embarked on wild, ardent love affairs.

She protests, says that eroticism is fatal.

That's part of the whole thing, Nanna replies calmly. That's the point. Without risks, eroticism would be nothing. So that's what they talk about. Not about her parents. They immerse themselves in eroticism as a bringer of life. As the origin of religion. As a protection against fossilizing and a tool for renewal.

It keeps her other thoughts at bay. She often calls in to see Nanna, and they tackle the extensive issue of love. Not the way girls usually do, by sharing their experiences. Thanks to the amount of reading Nanna has done, they approach eroticism through literature. She likes Nanna more and more each day.

Surrender, ecstasy, rapture.

To almost die, yet preserve oneself by not melting into the other person and being crushed. Nanna laughs — that's what eroticism is all about — and a funny little furrow appears between her eyes. She could have been an unbearable know-it-all, but she turns out to have a lighthearted and almost intrepid side: life seems to lie before her like a ripe fruit, just waiting for her to sink her teeth into it and take a bite.

Nanna reads D. H. Lawrence, and so does she.

She borrows *Lady Chatterley's Lover*, *Sons and Lovers*, and *Women in Love*, and reads them after Nanna. Lawrence regards a man and a woman as two supreme heavenly bodies. Two planets, separate and independent, faithfully following each other's orbits. Not crashing into each other. Not joining together. Simply following in each other's tracks, thanks to the laws of gravity.

Two heavenly bodies. Supreme. And equally strong. It is a relief to find images of love that are different from those to which she is exposed on a daily basis through a peephole into a marriage.

It transpires that Nanna was born in Stockholm too, and during her time at high school she has had her very own boat built at Möja. That's where the whole of her first student loan will be going.

A clinker-built motorboat. With a cabin and an Albin engine. That's where Nanna is going to spend the summer, with her poodle and her books and her typewriter. One hand on the tiller. Heading out toward the horizon. Alone and free.

As an overture to life, it is unbeatable.

• • •

Mom's contempt does not diminish, nor does her fury. It is an ancient female fury; she had no idea how extensive it was. It is archaic. It is like the fury of Medea, who killed her children to hurt her husband. Mom doesn't kill them. She simply draws the three sisters into her fury.

Which is terrible.

From Dad she moves on to all men.

Never trust a man. A mantra that becomes set in stone: *They should all be castrated, every last one of them, it's the only thing that will do any good.* She can understand the rage. What is more difficult to handle is Mom's low self-esteem.

The fact that Dad has left her proves that she is worthless. She dare not show herself on the street, where everyone would be able to see her limping as they gossip about the abandoned wife. The sisters are hauled into this feeling of worthlessness as if it were a fishing net. They never escape completely.

Not for the rest of their lives.

Ninne develops breathing difficulties. When she goes to bed she can't breathe, and thinks she is going to die. The girl doesn't dare tell Mom, but she calls Dad, who has rented a room in town. He takes Ninne to a doctor, who confirms the symptoms and says that she ought to move away from home. But Ninne is only fifteen and has several years left in school; where would she go?

I went to see Ricki, now when was that? Probably in early summer, after Granny and Granddad invited me to spend a few days at the market garden.

During my visit to Ricki I was so out of it that I hardly remember anything.

I wanted to know if Ricki was aware that Dad had left. I couldn't get the words out. I decided she did know, just like Laura and Grandpa. No one on my father's side of the family mentioned Mom anymore. Including Ricki. At Granny and Granddad's at that stage it was unthinkable even to mention Dad's existence.

They had loved him like a son.

Now he had been struck off the register. Persona non grata. I vaguely remember Olle coming into the living room with the boy trailing behind him; he had tucked a tea towel around his waist, and he called Ricki *precious Mommy* and wanted me to stay for dinner. The memory is diffuse.

But I couldn't possibly stay. I had to get back to Mom. The constant worry over her was eating away at me.

Ricki was so like my father. They both had a calmness and simplicity, but to care about them had almost become a betrayal of my mother.

I longed for light and simplicity, but the line between light and darkness ran right through me. No young person is experienced, and no child survives parental conflict without guilt. It's like *A Midsummer Night's Dream*, where the forces of nature are pitted against each other: Oberon, King of the Fairies, against Titania, Queen of the Fairies. Everything around them ends up out of joint.

She arrives home from a shift at the care home and can't bring herself to go upstairs. She lies down on the concrete floor of the bicycle storage room in the cellar. The barred windows let in a gray, woolly light. She has received a letter from Granny.

My darling eldest grandchild, I am so worried about your mother. You must take on the responsibility that your father has walked away from. I hear that Ia is being difficult — you must deal with her. I am relying on you. You have to take care of your mother.

She lies there in a kind of trance, the cold crawling into her spine.

Eventually she gets to her feet and goes upstairs, enclosed in her armor of cold indifference, and yet she is sick with worry about what she will face when she opens the door.

A couple of times, no more, when Mom keeps saying that she is going to kill herself, she calls Mom's old friend from the days when she studied music in Paris — Aunt Marta, who now lives in Lund.

She calls and Marta says, Hang on, I'm coming.

She stands at the kitchen window, her heart pounding. When she sees plump Marta turn the corner from Tellusgatan on her bicycle, the weight is lifted from her shoulders.

Aunt Marta is the only one who can calm Mom down. She persuades Mom to get dressed, places a pot of coffee on the kitchen table. She is the only adult who knows how hard it is to live inside Mom's despair. We sisters never discussed it between ourselves.

We just lived inside it.

． ． ．

Nanna calls and invites her downstairs. Her kind, gentle mom is out, and they knock back a bottle of wine, maybe two, and Nanna talks about why she and her mom came to Lund.

That is related to eroticism as well.

Before Nanna was born, her mom was married with three small children. When she met Nanna's father, who was also married, she was floored by a love that took her breath away. It was irresistible.

It was as if fate was giving her a command.

She split up from her first husband, took the three children, and married the love of her life. It was a scandal. And it turned out to be anything but an idyll.

Nanna's father was an alcoholic who abused her mother. Nanna and her half-siblings lived in fear. On one occasion he threatened them all with a gun. He was admitted to the psychiatric hospital at Beckomberga, but he was charm itself; he talked his way out and came back. He was just as jealous as before, and kept on hitting Nanna's mother.

This continued until Nanna was fourteen years old. Her mother woke at dawn one day; she had five precious minutes to gather up her most important belongings. They fled to Lund, hoping that Nanna's father wouldn't find out where they were.

But he tracked them down, and one day he rang the apartment.

Nanna was home alone, and took the call. When she heard who it was, her body became rigid. *It's me, it's Dad, say something.* Nanna knew she mustn't reveal where they were. She was so scared and lost for words that the colors in the rag rug started swapping over. Red became blue and blue became green.

The colors jumped around before her eyes, and she couldn't say a word. *Nanna, I know it's you, answer me.* She didn't know what to do with herself. *Say something, Nanna.* She hung up the phone. After that call her father disappeared without a trace. There was an appeal on the radio for information regarding his whereabouts.

Weeks and months passed, until a friend went out into the archipelago in his sailboat. It was late fall, and stormy. First the friend found the motorboat, smashed by the waves against a remote islet. Then he found the body. Nanna's father had shot himself with a Parabellum left over from his military service. The same gun he had once pointed at his family.

It is a story every bit as powerful as a Greek tragedy.

She stares at Nanna, lost for words. Nanna isn't crying, but she is taking fierce drags on her cigarette. The others might have been relieved, Nanna says, but not me. I missed him, but I couldn't let anyone see that.

It is a drama that penetrates her soul. The guilt, the loneliness, the feeling of missing someone. From that moment, Nanna becomes a really important person. All those years in school must be reassessed. The girl who caught up with her on her bicycle on Dalbyvägen. Who stood alone in the schoolyard with her book.

Who seemed arrogant and haughty, but who was lost and in despair. People don't know much about one another. She didn't know a thing about Nanna until now. Her own situation is nothing compared to what Nanna has gone through.

After that she becomes a part of Nanna's life. This enables her to escape her own life, and provides some relief. Nanna's life becomes a parallel existence to which she is allowed access, and it has the great advantage of belonging to someone else. But Nanna disappears to the archipelago and her boat with the Albin engine, while the girl gets a summer job at the Grand Hotel.

There too she lives as if she is in some kind of novel. It doesn't really concern her, but she can be in it and observe it greedily.

She is a cleaner, but also provides room service.

She receives a silver dollar from an elderly American who rings for tea, then opens the door stark naked. One man keeps ringing to ask her to brush his kaftan, or whatever the black cloak he wears is called. She kneels down and brushes the front, then the back, while he stands there with his eyes closed. When she has finished, he tells her to start again. She brushes away patiently, but when he wants her to do it for the third time, she tosses her head, hands him the brush, and leaves.

In the large attic room where traveling salesmen unpack their wares, things are a lot more straightforward. A ruddy-faced purveyor of ladies' underwear promises her a camisole, a pair of panties, and a slip if she is a little bit nice to him. He chases her around the table waving a camisole; she only just manages to get away, laughing hysterically as she runs down the stairs.

The kitchen is in the basement, and from halfway down the stairs where she enters the orders she can watch the staff on either side of the table, chopping and slicing and dicing. They work like lightning. The fattest person has her wedding and engagement rings fixed to her chest with a safety pin, jingling in time with her knife. She lingers for a moment to listen to the shouting.

In the cleaners' storeroom where they have coffee, she hears all the gossip about the guests while the most athletic cleaner practices her gymnastics on the floor. There's plenty to take in: how couples behave, what they leave behind on the sheets.

Bodily fluids, wine stains, blood and excrement.

She works with a middle-aged woman who keeps inviting her home. This is her first lesbian approach. It's a bit sad to have to say no, because the woman is very nice, and teaches her useful tricks — like wiping glasses with a used hand towel, which is much quicker than taking them all the way down to the kitchen to wash and bringing them back up again.

In every room, in the beds she makes, in the bathrooms where she mops the floor, countless dramas have been played out. Her future is uncertain, and she fears it. But she thinks she could probably run a small hotel herself, creating a backdrop for breakups, passion, and suicide.

A hotel is a novel with no ending. As she cycles home in the twilight the darkness falls inside her, and the walls become porous once more.

Then she steps into Nanna's life, into some as yet unlit episode, or along some horrific but strangely reassuring sidetrack in the story of the girl whose father shot himself with a Parabellum.

∙ ∙ ∙

She can't stand it any longer. So she takes off with her former classmate Monki. She carries out the maneuver so skillfully that her mother is taken unawares.

It's just a short trip, after all. She'll be back soon. They put on their student caps (it's the last time she wears hers) and hitch to Paris; they are there in three or four days. Without having been raped. Or robbed.

Just laughed at a few times because of their caps; the Germans and the French don't seem to understand what they mean.

They find a cheap hotel on the rue Dauphine not far from the Pont Neuf. Five francs a night, but only three if you share *un grand lit*. Which they do. However, after a short time Monki leaves her to take up a job as a waitress in Spain.

She stays on alone in the crap hotel room. What is she supposed to do in Paris? She hasn't a clue. She doesn't know anyone. The rusty faucet drips slowly into the basin. She washes her feet in it, picks up her sketch pad and goes out.

Her idea is that she is in Paris to *absorb the atmosphere, expand her senses,* and *gain new impressions.*

Loneliness plods patiently along beside her. She isn't entirely present, and has no need to fear it. In a museum she draws ancient Roman statues. She gets into the habit of dropping in to see an Armenian who runs a gallery; he is an elegant gentleman who offers her mint tea.

She finds her way to the Musée de l'homme, where she meets the stuffed Hottentot woman, much to her surprise. Actually, she isn't stuffed, the exhibit is a cast. A naked black woman with huge buttocks. Exotic. But still a woman.

How can they put a woman on display? She is shaken. She visits the museum several times; she sits on the floor in front of the woman and draws her.

She has no intention of ever forgetting this woman.

The evenings, most evenings, she spends at the Tabou jazz club, long ago abandoned by Juliette Gréco. However, there is good modern jazz on offer, and soon all the staff seem to recognize her. Like the melancholy Monsieur Moustache, for example, so called because of his drooping black mustache. He serves her many glasses of red wine and forgets to take her money.

There is no plan behind any of it. And the future is a hole.

She doesn't do anything in particular. That's not quite true — she works her way through a novel by Albert Camus. Then a few more. Occasionally she takes out her notebook containing math problems. She is thinking that she ought to complement her arts studies with the scientific side. In order to become something. A doctor, maybe.

Or an architect, like Ricki. She stares gloomily at the math problems and realizes that she will never be able to solve them. After a while she throws the book into the garbage can, which stinks of tobacco. Just a short trip? The weeks pass. Without her noticing how it happens, she gets trapped in Paris.

She is neither happy nor unhappy. She drifts around. She sits in cafés. She receives the stream of people coming toward her. White, black, Asians and Arabs: the river that never dries up in the violet light of evening.

During the day: with her sketch pad in the Jardin du Luxembourg among the birds and the trees. In the evening: the metallic smell of the Métro. The beggars. The poverty in the back streets.

She inhales the smells of greasy food, sweat, and oblivion. Paris is a perfect counterpart to the emptiness inside her; it makes no demands. Nothing hurts her. She is trapped in Paris as if she were in a dream. It is a flight.

As if life itself isn't a flight. Perhaps it is more about being present. She contemplates the glittering water as it gushes down the gutters. She leans against the stones of the Pont Neuf and gazes at the barges down below. She can watch the children playing in the streets around the rue Dauphine for hours.

From her window in the hotel room she looks down on the courtyard at the back. It is raining. A man is dancing, holding an umbrella over a woman who is sweeping the yard. The woman is singing, and the man dances like a bird.

She isn't happy, but she is grateful for the opportunity to be alone.

She reaches out for words, trying to grab hold of them. Lying on her stomach in bed, it is night and the bedside lamp is buzzing as usual. The words flock around her. Some are kind, others scornful. Every word has its own form. And they keep her company.

Not because she writes them down. She simply allows them to come. The man with the umbrella and the woman with her broom, singing. That could have been a possibility. To try to write about it. She doesn't do it.

Nor does she pay any heed to time. In the morning when she wakes, she lies in bed watching the dust motes swirling in a ray of sunlight from the window. A thousand tiny, dancing fragments. She thinks she has never seen anything more beautiful. Yet another day awaits her, another blank canvas.

On one such day as she gazes blankly at the window of a shoe shop on the rue Montmartre, she is addressed by an enormous, coal-black man. He has kind eyes, and is smartly dressed in a suit and tie.

His French is easy to understand. He is studying law, and comes from Senegal — just like the poet Léopold Senghor, who has written about *négritude*. She has read some of his poems.

The man invites her to a café. They talk about racial segregation, a topic that interests her greatly. While they are sitting at the table, a breathtakingly beautiful couple walk by. A woman with red hair like Rita Hayworth, and a slender black man in glasses, with a scarf nonchalantly wound around his neck.

They are so terribly beautiful that it hurts. Even her nipples and her sex hurt. In Paris a black person and a white person can live together, her companion says, but that's not true of many other places in Europe.

He claims to be the son of a chief with seven wives. She doesn't believe him, but he assures her that it's true. They see each other again. He asks her to visit him in his hotel room.

She laughs and tells him that she has a fiancé. But they see each other again. And he proposes to her.

That makes her laugh even more. Won't he be going back home to Senegal? What would she do there? He maintains that as his European wife, she would be able to do whatever she wanted. Paint, write poetry, run a nightclub, get to know the country, or simply relax. It is no problem whatsoever.

And yes, she believes him.

They stroll along the streets and through the parks. He puts his arm around her shoulders. She can't marry him, because she isn't in love with him. But that's not a problem either. He can make her fall in love with him through magic, he says. In order to achieve this he takes photographs of her in front of monuments and churches, and asks for a strand of her hair and a nail clipping.

He is going to post everything to the shaman in his village, and swears that she will soon be besotted by him. Although she has a number of issues, they evaporate in his presence. Senegal — why not?

They are sitting in the sunshine with a pastis in the Place de la Contrescarpe. He has sent the package to his village, but unfortunately she hasn't fallen in love. She smiles at him and his shaman.

Just you wait, he says, straightening his tie.

But what if she does fall in love and they get married, would she be expected to share him with a whole heap of wives? Her friend throws back his head and laughs out loud.

What does she think? He's a modern African!

He is the only person she gets to know well in Paris. He is intelligent, childlike, warmhearted. And she is curious about the shaman's capabilities. Shamanism is about the influence of the spirits, the effect they can have. She thinks she knows something about all that. Sometimes she is already in Senegal.

That isn't her, of course. It is an eighteen-year-old woman who has broken away from everything and nothing. She has nothing against the idea, and yet it really doesn't concern her. When they don't see each other, she forgets about him, but when she is on her way to their next meeting, she looks forward to it. She is not in love. If she were to go with him to Senegal, and if he were to acquire six more wives, she wouldn't be jealous, for that simple reason.

It would suit her perfectly. Him too, presumably. They would follow each other's orbits like two supreme planets. They would not destroy or annihilate each other. She is excited, enjoying being alone in Paris.

•   •   •

However, she receives an unexpected telephone call at the hotel, and is summoned down to take it by Madame la concierge. The dinosaur in the scruffy little office has no intention of leaving her alone.

It turns out that Mom is on her way, along with Aunt Marta; Mom is treating her to the trip. She books a double room for them at her hotel, the Hôtel des Grands Balcons, which in spite of its stylish name lacks both large and small balconies. If they find the room too basic, they can always move to a better hotel.

Mom loves Paris. The fact that she wants to come is a good sign. But in the hotel room once they have arrived: utter despair. Tears, booze, curses. Even calm, steady Aunt Marta doesn't know what to do.

The girl hasn't forgotten her mother's unhappiness, she has simply taken a little break from it. However, Mom's view is that they have come to take her home. Five weeks in Paris, or is it six, and what has she actually been doing?

She finds it difficult to answer. She didn't have any kind of plan for her stay. She hasn't studied the language, she has merely picked her way through a few books with the aid of a pocket dictionary. Stood reading in bookshops and at the stalls of the *bouquinistes* along the banks of the Seine. Trotted around museums and galleries. She has walked miles and miles. Hundreds of paintings in the Louvre, with elements of light and shadow. A language where nothing is absolute.

She has drawn. She has wandered the streets for hours. She has visited the cast of that defenseless woman several times. She has spent many evenings hanging out at Tabou. She doesn't mention this, or her Senegalese friend. You can't just drift around, Mom states firmly, without listening. And it's true, she has to admit it: she hasn't done anything in particular.

She hasn't thought about the future. She hasn't set a date for her return home. They go out to eat at a depressing place, and Mom keeps on badmouthing Dad.

Once again she is caught up in Mom's unhappiness. Mom's reality is stone, a heavy weight, incontrovertibility. But it is insulting to be dragged home against her will. Humiliating. Everything within her rises up in protest. She sees herself through her mother's eyes: a young girl, thoughtless and fickle. That too is an insult.

Mom doesn't have room for anyone but herself.

That's the way it has always been, but now it has been reinforced by the misery Dad has heaped upon her. She doesn't believe Mom has come to take her home. Mom has come because she couldn't stand being at home. She has been driven here by sorrow. This is not the moment to discuss motives, and she must keep the realization to herself.

It is the communicating vessel.

Refusing to cooperate with Mom would involve disregarding her pain. She promises to go home with Mom and Aunt Marta. She gives assurances, makes promises. And as she does so the past few weeks fade away.

The lack of demands. The sparkling mornings. The blue twilight. The man dancing beneath an umbrella. Everything, including time's capacity to remain outside of time, and the thoughts that are not thoughts but feelings and poetry, a form of writing that is not written, and those powerful sensory impressions — all of it is diluted and dispersed.

One thing she absolutely insists on: she is going to see her Senegalese friend one last time. This causes a scene in Mom and Marta's hotel room. Who is this guy? Mom stares at her.

A *Negro*? She really is on a downward slope.

She leaves rue Dauphine feeling much more upset than she would like to be. It is raining. Yellow leaves float along the surface of the Seine. They have arranged to meet at an Ethiopian restaurant. They eat, and afterward it rains even more heavily and she goes back to his nearby hotel room.

Before they walk through the main door she tells him that she has no intention of going to bed with him. He nods, of course not; she is just sheltering from the rain.

They are greeted by *la concierge*, a bleached blonde who taps on the reception desk with a coin. No women in the room. The wrinkled blonde and the man from Senegal negotiate, quietly at first and then increasingly loudly, until he presses something, presumably a banknote, into her hand.

The woman still shouts after them as they walk up the stairs; the girl doesn't understand what she says, but it is obviously something rude and disparaging.

His hotel room is as sparse as hers. There is nowhere to sit except on the bed. He quickly removes his clothes. Before he closes the curtains, she sees how amazing his body is.

Dazzling. More beautiful than any of the Roman statues she has sketched. He lies down on top of her.

She protests a little. Not very much.

His tongue, his soft fingers. He is panting, repeating *jouissance, la jouissance*, a word that is as lovely as his body. Let us give each other pleasure, do not deny us *un peu de jouissance*.

That word — she has never forgotten it. He touches her everywhere, she touches him. She has no protection and is afraid, but he chivalrously withdraws and spurts his seed over her stomach. She listens to the rain hammering on the windowpane, inside herself, everywhere. In her mind's eye she sees Mom and Marta, waiting.

The image is washed away by the water.

They make love again as the water flows through time, through the years, splashing and gushing and forming whirlpools and waterfalls. This is her last night in Paris, and the hours and days behind her are carried along with the river, flowing down to the sea.

The whole of her time in Paris rushes away so that she can be transported home like a parcel, a knapsack. Her friend just wants to keep on going, but she can't stay. After all, eventually she will have to go.

We won't see each other again.

Mais si. Many times. We will see each other very often.

Non. I am leaving tomorrow.

When he understands what she is saying, there is no reasoning with him. He holds on to her. Won't let her go. She has to push him hard, almost fight with him to get out of bed. He throws himself on his back and repeats that they will see each other again.

He falls asleep. In the darkness she gropes for the most important items of clothing and puts them on. She avoids looking at the dragon at reception, but can feel the woman's harsh eyes on her back as the door closes behind her.

The streets are shining. From the treetops high above, the heavy scent of burgeoning greenery drifts down. This is hers and hers alone: those past few hours and this leisurely stroll back to the hotel. At least there are a few things in life that are hers and no one else's.

She leans against the rough stones of the Pont Neuf. She stands there for a long time. Down below her the River Seine, fast-moving gray waves with a pigeon-blue shimmer. Glimmers of light enveloped in moisture are reflected in the water. She has no negative feelings toward him.

She does have negative feelings about the rest of it: the journey home, Mom's attempt to blackmail her, the imprisonment that is waiting for her. But Mom's incarceration is worse. Mom is trapped in a horrible sense of loss, an amputation, an incomprehensible humiliation. In spite of everything, the girl has at least had a breathing space.

During the journey home she picks up fragments of the conversation between Mom and Marta. *A Negro, what a little fool she is.* Marta tries to speak up on her behalf, but there is no point. It is mortifying, not least being dragged home like this.

Sometimes she really hates her mother.

But she tells herself that she is going home voluntarily, so that Mom's misery won't be compounded. So that she won't be hurt anymore.

Their train arrives in Travemünde. She has been here before. With a German family in a blue Volkswagen. She was fifteen years old. That was in a completely different life. The tickets for the ferry have all gone. Every hotel is fully booked.

Eventually they find overnight accommodation in a trailer park by the shore. Summer is over, and the rain hammers down on the metal roof of their trailer. Mom sits slumped over her bad leg. Everything is dreadful. They are saved by Marta's unfailing good humor.

Plump Marta squelches away in the rain and charms the park supervisor, returning with schnapps to cheer everyone up. And it actually works. Even Mom has to smile at their situation.

After the schnapps Marta insists on going for a swim. They walk together down to the long, sandy beach. It is dark and deserted, and the waves are like three-story buildings — black and shining, tipped with foaming white. As they reach the shore they settle down to a sighing swell.

They stand on the shore gazing out across the waves. Behind them they can just make out the misty lights from the windows of the trailers, but on the shore they are alone. And Marta raises her arms toward the sky and salutes the sea.

It is like some magnificent pagan ritual.

The whole thing is completely crazy. The journey home is a schizophrenic symphony by a deranged artist. Marta hurls herself into the water with a deafening roar, wallowing like a whale, while the girl swims with rain above her head and in her hair and her mouth. Marta puffs and pants and they yell to each other across the swells, and she might as well make the best of things.

•   •   •

Dad's room is unprepossessing. She looks around. A desk, a bed, outside the room two hotplates and a sink. He hugs her and takes her coat, and even though it is new and strange — so *this* is where he lives now? — she feels welcome. Planks of wood propped up on bricks serve as bookshelves.

His cups and plates don't match, but as usual his desk is piled high with papers covered with scribbled formulas, lovely curves and symbols that she doesn't understand. The most beautiful mathematical solution is the simplest, Dad often says. That could be a motto for the way he lives his life.

Simplest is best. Mathematics has its own particular beauty.

Crystalline. Beyond human suffering. Visiting him in his new life is a bit like meeting a stranger, even though she knows him so well. And besides, it's not just his new life, it's everyone's; a cog has slid across another cog and everything has switched to a different track, and now it's like this.

Can you work properly here? I guess so, Dad replies. I'm with John Steinbeck. You carefully sharpen all your pencils, you arrange your papers in perfect order, in a neat and tidy pile, you place a steaming cup of coffee beside you and light the first cigarette of the morning, then you open yourself to great inspiration.

At that moment your thoughts flap around like giddy hens in a farmyard, and you can't grab hold of a single one of them. She bursts out laughing.

That's how Dad provided solace, joked away all her troubles and woes and restored a sense of proportion in the blink of an eye, which means realizing that one's own life isn't the main issue. Never run after a streetcar or a boy, there will always be another one along in a minute. That's Dad. A shrug and a kindly, ironic grimace as he allows the world to take care of itself.

Everything will always sort itself out. No reason to panic. Tomorrow is another day. This attitude has provided a defense against chaos, inner tumult, and panic. And yet, even though he is so unsuited to catastrophe, to imbalance, to exaggeration, this potentially good aspect of his character has left the family and himself in a state of disarray, uncertainty, and total flux.

It is a paradox. And it is impossible to talk about it.

At a student union event she danced with one of his students, a blond guy with clever eyes. *Your dad is the most considerate person I've ever met, he seems incapable of being mean.* Really? she says, sounding surprised.

Dad's student nods and says that her father reminds him of a boy, slightly impatient. Your dad is incredibly kind, he reiterates.

Is he? Mom takes the opposite view. Inconsiderate, fawning, a liar. She needs her father. She doesn't want to take sides. She doesn't want to choose.

Her rare visits allow her to see new sides of her father. On one occasion he tells her about a dream he had that morning.

He doesn't remember the details, just that he woke surrounded and lifted up by a bright light.

It was almost *spiritual*, he says, sounding quite overcome.

Does he have religious feelings? That would be unlike him. She decides that he is experiencing a sense of liberation because he has moved out and left them. On another visit a pigeon has laid her eggs in the guttering outside his only window. He won't open it for fear of disturbing her. He is very fond of the pigeon, he says.

The pigeon is company for him in his loneliness.

He doesn't just feel liberated, he is also lonely. Apparently. It's only natural. After all, they have always been a pentagram, the five of them.

All three sisters visit him, but never together. One at a time, and without telling Mom. From Ia she learns that the relationship with Vibeke is still going on. Ia finds her way to Dad's room after school, seeking peace and quiet. Which is much needed.

One day when she is there, the phone rings. Ia can hear that it's Vibeke, as clearly as if she were in the room. *I'll meet you in fifteen minutes at the usual place.* And suddenly Dad is in a hurry. The call came from the university department, he claims, he has forgotten about an important meeting and he has to leave right away. So Ia cycles home.

Dad tells lies, Ia states, with a thirteen-year-old's tone of slight disappointment and arrogance. As if she were commenting on an area that had been hit by a natural disaster. She adds that everything is perfectly normal at home with

Vibeke and Bertil. The catastrophe appears to have struck only this family.

A localized storm, as they say on the radio.

Dad sticks to a casual, carefree approach. Digging deeper is not something he's interested in. Psychology isn't his thing. Presumably he is skeptical about it. She isn't about to accuse him of anything. During her visits they chat about superficial matters: a book, a movie, a newspaper article.

He thinks she ought to choose something to study at the university, but she's not interested in anything.

She is living in limbo, like a particle flung around in a void. Sometimes she fears for her sanity. Mom's outbursts make her feel worthless. There are moments when she simply wants to die.

She can't say that kind of thing to Dad. She can't say anything that might sound hysterical, make him feel uncomfortable, make him turn away in silence as he has turned away from Mom. They never talk about Mom. Dad doesn't ask about her.

And she doesn't want to expose Mom's humiliation, which is how she sees it. It is mortifying for Mom to be forced to question everything in her life, herself most of all, and to trample around in a boggy mess of rage, vicious words, and despair. He ought to know — he lived with her for long enough.

But he doesn't ask, which means that she avoids key topics, such as how he views the future. Whether he is intending to move back home. In her calmer moments, Mom hopes that will happen. This is a crisis, violent and long-lasting, admittedly, but it will pass. And who knows.

But Dad says nothing. Sometimes it seems to her that he believes his daughters *know everything and that there is no need for explanations.* But they know nothing!

If only he could come right out with it, say that he found himself in an impossible situation. Say whether he wanted Vibeke or not. Say that he is never coming home, or that he hopes to return — anything, just so long as they know.

But he says nothing. Her parents remain married. It also seems as if it's going to stay that way. Unresolved, in other words.

Dad speaks on a personal level on only one occasion. Well, almost personal. He asks — unexpectedly — if she remembers the statue of the naked woman outside the minimarket in Årsta. She does. Mom slipped on the ice and fell right in front of that statue. And Dad says that every time he walked past that naked woman, he was seized by such a strong sense of unease that he could hardly bring himself to go home.

He doesn't understand it, he says. For once he looks troubled. It's as if he wants her to understand it for him.

First thought: he's thinking of Mom. Of her body. His obligations toward her. His sexual obligation. Men are repulsed by the female body. They find the female body's emissions and blood disgusting, but are forced to go there by the male sex drive. A masochistic thought that also strikes her.

With a certain amount of effort, she manages to shake it off.

He has Vibeke. It is Mom's body that revolts him. That's what he says. At that moment she feels sick. He is sharing a confidence that has nothing to do with her, a confidence that should not be shared with a nineteen-year-old daughter. She is angry.

But Dad drops the subject and never returns to it again. She realizes that he is facing something he *really doesn't understand*. Did he feel inadequate when he was with Mom? Probably. Was that why he left? Maybe.

He seems to spend a lot of time brooding about himself and his role. He doesn't appear to want to break away from Mom. It is possible that she's right, that they really do belong together. If only Mom could avoid getting stuck in her putrefaction, in her rage and her contempt, if she could just accept him and forgive him, then maybe things could work out.

That's what she thinks. Sometimes. At the beginning.

During the first three or four years.

In spite of everything, visiting Dad means experiencing a little bit of stability. It is also somewhat ambivalent and ambiguous, because he doesn't say anything. He doesn't say whether he's waiting for Vibeke to get a divorce. Or whether he wants to come back to Mom, and is just biding his time until the right moment comes along. Or whether he's fine as he is.

He doesn't say a word about Mom.

Ever. He takes Ninne on a trip to Paris. He invites Ia to Copenhagen, where he works as a lecturer for a while. He unexpectedly gives the girl a dress that is nicer than any she has ever owned. He lives in his little room when he isn't lecturing overseas.

He travels all the way to Africa to teach.

Ambivalence means wanting two things at the same time. Loving and hating simultaneously, for example. And the strange part is that although the ambivalence is her father's, it moves in and occupies her. Never being able to make up her mind. Constantly worrying about upsetting someone. Which means she can't create her own shape.

A demarcation line against others. But time passes. Year follows year, and nothing changes. The ambivalence digs down deeper inside her.

Until it is as deep as the Mariana Trench.

• • •

The ice down below the house on Yxlan formed a bobbing mass at first, then froze solid. Now it is beginning to break up. Ice floes that have been torn loose are floating northward, with ducks and swans standing on top of them, grabbing a free ride.

They look funny. Do they know where they're going?

I have been in town a few times and have come back here. The sun is showing its face with increasing frequency. Spring is on its way. It is unclear what actually happens when decisions are made in the skein of tangled threads of which life is currently made up.

Decisions are seldom made with logic and clear thinking.

If it seems that way, it is usually because we have put a spin on the situation afterward. A wise person once said that we consist only of fiction, of the idea we construct about ourselves. Sometimes it seems to me that the story I am telling about myself — about her — all those years ago has been cobbled together into a fossilized memory, which has gradually changed as she became me.

We rattle around inside the armor of memory.

Many of the people about whom I write are dead. They cannot defend themselves, they are at the mercy of a young girl whom I sometimes cannot distinguish from myself.

Can I discover something new? I am sticking to the questions she asked when she was young. The first question: what is truth? The second: love. Where does love go when it dies? The third: what do you do to be able to be yourself?

We are fiction. We create ourselves with words. This is my fiction: I perceived my father as unbearably indecisive. I could have been wrong.

But I kept all options open in all directions.

By doing so I allowed everything to pass through me, and lost myself. I got the idea that Dad was waiting for something. For what? If one of them could just make a decision, I thought back then. If Mom could give up expecting him to come back. If Dad could ask for a divorce.

Then the world could start turning again and I would be able to escape, get away. Apply for a place at art school, make a movie, become a doctor in Africa. Or get a job on a boat and head off anywhere, or maybe to Indonesia where apparently I had quite a few relatives — that was just a fraction of the thoughts that went through my mind, all equally unrealistic.

I waited, but they didn't make any decisions.

According to later witness accounts, this is what really happened. When we arrived in Lund, Dad and Vibeke instantly fell in love.

That's what Vibeke wrote in a letter to Laura, which we found in Laura's apartment after her death. According to Vibeke, Dad took off his wedding ring back in 1948. They knew immediately that they were meant for each other. They shared the same lust for life, but they had both married the wrong person.

And Laura told me — after my father's death — that he had confided in her. For the sake of his children, he had to stay and try to endure his marriage. I'm counting the days and the years, he had said to Laura, until the children are old enough. He worked hard to avoid having to think.

The third account is from my father's second wife, also after his death. When he arrived in Lund in 1952, the sexual side of his marriage was already at an end. He was sexually famished. I need someone, anyone, he thought, and that someone happened to be Vibeke.

If you put these three accounts into a pot and shake them up, you get a more or less consistent picture, albeit with quite a lot of gaps. My fiction today: my father was a nice man who didn't want to hurt anyone.

But he believed he had obligations. To Vibeke. And to Bertil, a close friend who must be kept in the dark. And to Mom, to whom — I am convinced of this — he was still emotionally tied, in spite of everything. He was very attached to his daughters. He had left us, and he was caught up in a tangle of interwoven obligations; he couldn't see a way out. He allowed one day after another to pass.

Mathematics was a refuge and a solace.

When many years had passed, I wrote a letter to my father. I told him how we had dangled in that state of uncertainty he had created. If he had no intention of going back to Mom, why didn't he get a divorce? I was caught up in that uncertainty.

So were my sisters, I think. We fell in love with the wrong kind of men, those who seemed ambivalent. Ambivalence is a major force in eroticism. We were attracted to men who didn't know what they wanted. Who were already in a relationship. Who were unable to break free.

Who couldn't make up their minds. That's what happened to me, anyway.

I wrote to my father and tried to explain all this to him. Of course that says something about me, the fact that I waited for a decision on their part before I felt I was free to make a decision of my own. So many lost years. My father was, as you might expect, annoyed. He didn't want anyone interfering in his life.

I replied that his life was other people's lives too, and that I didn't want to see him until he had made a decision that would put an end to the quagmire that had paralyzed us all. I tried to put it politely, and without badmouthing Mom.

It was the summer of 1966, just over eight years after he had left us. In the fall he asked for a divorce, through his lawyer. I felt I could take a certain amount of credit for that. Maybe I was wrong. Mom hit rock bottom once more. It is possible that my letter had no effect, but at the time I thought my parents had ended up in a state of permanent inertia. Paralysis. Constantly putting things off.

They saw each other, he came round for dinner and cycled back to his room. He always spent Christmas Eve with us, which was pure torture. Then he headed off again, slightly the worse for wear. It was many years before I understood the power my father's silence had exerted.

Oh yes, the obstinate silence of men. But something happened after my letter. He finally made a decision. Just before he asked Mom for a divorce, he finished with Vibeke. That emerged in her letter to Laura.

Vibeke missed him desperately, she wrote. She and Bertil had just ended their marriage, an ugly and bitter divorce, she wrote. But my father abandoned her too, in order to marry a third woman.

She was a door that opened for him; he was able to walk out through that door and leave the whole mess behind him. That's my perception, anyway. I never discussed it with my father. Nor have I ever managed to make up my mind as to whether the whole thing is a rather banal tale, or one that is a little unusual because of the amount of time it covered. I tend toward the latter view.

Following the divorce, my parents didn't see each other again. Not for thirty years. Not until just before my father's death, when he was in the hospital and in a bad way.

All of a sudden he desperately wanted to see Mom.

He was like a man possessed. It's the only time I ever experienced such an unshakable resolve in my father. He refused to give up, and he begged me to help him. Mom, who hadn't had a good word to say about him through all those years, wasn't surprised when I asked her if she would come visit him.

I've been expecting it, she said. I know he wants to see me.

As if it were entirely self-evident.

I drove her to the hospital and they met. He sat on a chair in front of an elevator door that was constantly opening and closing, with an overflowing ashtray beside him. Mom sat on a chair opposite him. The meeting lasted for maybe twenty minutes. I have written about it in *A Winter in Stockholm*. They were old.

I was afraid that Mom would come out with all the bad stuff she had said and thought about him over the years. I needn't have worried. They smoked. She leaned forward and lit his cigarette for him. They didn't talk about anything in particular. They looked at each other, and were very kind to each other.

For me: a genuine miracle. Then a nurse came to fetch him. That's what happened. It was the last time they met, and it was good. Something was concluded, for them and for me. He died not long afterward.

• • •

My problem was how to get out. Or rather, how do you find your way into life? You never stop doing that, not until you stop breathing. *Anywhere out of this world*, as Edgar Allan Poe wrote. I changed it to *Anywhere at all, but into this world* in my rented room at the time.

The second winter after graduating from high school, and she has gotten to know a Danish painter and ceramic artist who offers board and lodgings in exchange for her taking care of the household and his four small children. She will also have the opportunity to learn the secrets of ceramics.

He has a summer cottage in Vikhög on the coast.

The artist's wife is slim, with long legs; she is breastfeeding her newborn baby. The girl often walks on the shore, where swans have blown in. She writes poetry in her head. *The gale robs me of my voice.* Everyone has a story into which they can fit their life. She ought to take her place in her own story, but she doesn't have one. *The wind steals my cries away from me.*

In the evenings when the children are asleep, they sit in the kitchen and the artist talks about the war, when he worked for the Resistance. His wife talks about a prophet called Hubbard who has created a doctrine known as Scientology, and who has seen through the lies of the bourgeois society. As have the artist and his wife.

All three of them read Henry Miller. The other two get excited — sperm, piss, excrement — but she finds Miller dull. The artist is constantly trying to get her into bed. His wife doesn't mind, he claims. They could have lots of fun in bed, the three of them.

That's their attitude to life — rebelling against convention.

In principle she would like to share this view, but she finds him exhausting. He never stops talking — in his studio, in the kitchen, in the woodshed. She doesn't want to share a bed with him and his wife. He can't understand it. He wants to have a serious conversation with her.

He has reached the conclusion that she lacks contact with her *inner life*. Oh yes, and how exactly does he know this?

After the conversation she is so annoyed that she loads the kiln carelessly, and several of his thin mugs are ruined. She *does* have an inner life; she just can't reach it. There is something in the way. But isn't that exactly what he's saying?

He is furious about the disastrous firing and calls her *indolent, uninterested*, and *indifferent*. He's right. She apologizes. They have a woodshed with books scattered all over the floor; she goes and sits in there and reads poems by Poe and Rilke to get some peace and quiet and to calm down. The artist turns straight back to the sexual pressurization. She is tired of having to come up with arguments to explain why she doesn't want to do it.

He thinks he has the right to demand reasons, which is both trying and taxing. And if the argument is not good enough in his opinion, he draws conclusions about her *inner life*. Who does he think he is?

She doesn't dislike him or his wife. On the contrary, they are kind and, in their own way, respectful; life with them is a sort of blessed asylum. She admires his pottery when it comes out of the kiln. She also strips naked and models for him. It costs her nothing.

She does some painting in Lund, but is seized by a sense of emptiness. She doesn't know what she's doing. She sits in front of the mirror and doesn't recognize her face.

If anyone had suggested she was depressed, she would have been astonished. Depression — that means electric shocks and paranoia. She is simply gray inside, like cement. She grits her teeth. She can't be a painter, she lacks the talent.

Ceramics might be a possibility. If every life is a story, the pot can be seen as a container for life.

That's the way she tries to think.

She receives a letter from her Senegalese friend. He has looked on the map to see where Lund is, and suggests they should meet in Copenhagen. She has almost forgotten him, and is charmed by the fact that he remembers her. But the shaman's magic hasn't worked, and she doesn't reply to the letter.

She travels between Vikhög and Lund. She tries to be nice to Mom. This is what she can do, shoulder the responsibility Dad has walked away from. She isn't nice at all. She has simply ended up in the middle of something that means her lust for life is chewed to pieces by a machine with iron teeth so that it runs through her fingers like shingle and gravel.

There were many obstacles for a girl like her: being kind, sympathetic, empathetic. At the same time she had to wriggle out of the unceasing sexual pressure — it was like trying to get through a dense hedge of demands — but without hurting anyone.

Not only pressure from the artist. A constant whining and nagging from men who couldn't cope with rejection. She feels guilty because she thinks she ought to be able to do something for her parents, which is unreasonable. Perhaps no one is asking such a thing of her, but that's what she's gotten into her head. She feels guilty about the person she is.

She can be seen through the binoculars turned the wrong way around — closer this time.

One winter evening she bumps into Dad on Lilla Fiskaregatan. This makes her indescribably happy. She is on her way to the cinema, and he joins her: *L'Avventura*, by Michelangelo Antonioni, with Monica Vitti. He falls asleep during the short feature. She tries to wake him with a strong Tenor lozenge, but it goes down the wrong way and he has such a violent coughing fit that she is grateful when he falls asleep again.

Alain Resnais's short feature shows images from a recently liberated concentration camp. Barbed wired. Prisoners and dead bodies. And Germans, forced to visit by the Allies, standing there with handkerchiefs pressed to their noses. It is only ten years since she took a language course in Lübeck. She is pushed down in her seat by indignation, sorrow, and guilt.

The main movie shows Vitti in dark towns, treeless landscapes, and whitewashed rooms. She doesn't have the energy to follow the plot, but the actress's face absorbs the distress from the first film. When it is over she is blinded by tears, and has to stay in her seat letting everyone else pass by while she pulls herself together.

And when she has pulled herself together, she wakes Dad.

He invites her to a café for a sandwich, then he asks—very tactfully—what she is actually doing in Vikhög, is she thinking of becoming an *artist*? He sounds skeptical. An artist? She defends herself. The word is too big. She just wants to get rid of the blockage, the plug inside her that is stopping her from living.

She tells him that ceramics is an interim project, halfway to art but less pretentious: it's just making pots. If she had been honest she would have said that she wanted to avoid living. She didn't want to die, exactly, but she did want to avoid living. You don't say that sort of thing to your dad. Who seems tired this evening.

You can't stay in Vikhög looking after kids for the rest of your life! He sounds unexpectedly opinionated.

And what about you? she snaps back. How long are you going to stay in that pathetic little room—the rest of your life?

For the time being, Dad answers tersely. He doesn't expand on the situation, but he does tell her that Ricki is sick. They are standing on Södergatan, she is leaning on her bicycle. Tiny ice crystals are drifting down from the sky. Don't leave me, Daddy! She doesn't shout out those words. She doesn't even say them. She simply asks what's wrong with Ricki.

He doesn't know. He says he's sure she'll be fine.

The snowflakes land on his white hair. He turns up his collar and walks away, heading for his little room. She stands there watching him go, until he disappears among the trees in Lundagård. Then she cycles home. Where Mom is waiting.

Wide awake and inconsolable.

• • •

The suction drags her down, inexorably downward. She leaves the Danish artist and Vikhög. She becomes an apprentice with the ceramicist Signe Persson-Melin in Malmö. On the train between Lund and Malmö she reads the books she has borrowed from Nanna, who has been studying philosophy. *The Ways of Thought*, by Gunnar Aspelin.

The Problems of Philosophy, by Bertrand Russell. *Philosophy in a New Key*, by Susan Langer. Outside the train window she sees figures in transparent spheres, desperately fighting to get out. Spheres containing trapped souls, hovering above grotesque scenery. Where has she seen them — in a painting by Hieronymus Bosch? But the spheres outside the window are not soap bubbles. They are resistant cages made of a material that is harder than hard. She is locked inside such a cage. She despises herself for it, but that's the way it is.

Sitting at a potter's wheel that goes round and round, and it takes ten years to become a fully trained potter? Ten years! To learn how to repeat shapes so that they are all exactly the same.

She unceremoniously abandons ceramics.

She rents a room in town so that she can study philosophy. She can't live at home. The downward pull is too strong there. But she doesn't turn her back on them. She cycles home to

Mom, who needs her. And maybe, although I didn't think of this until much later — maybe I needed a mother too.

The rented room is on a corridor outside a ladies' hair salon. It stinks of perming solution. She goes into the kitchen to make a cup of coffee, and she can see into the salon. Fine ladies are sitting under the dryers looking like astronauts, some with a little dog on their lap.

She christens all the little dogs Laika. After the dog who met her demise in the *Sputnik* spacecraft. She hopes things will go better for these little dogs. Her boyfriend comes to visit her in the smelly room. He's the one who gave her a ride home on his bicycle after the graduation party; he is now studying at Chalmers.

They make love in the narrow bed. It is friendly. Often ecstatic. She is scared of getting pregnant, but he keeps her in the world, as Nanna does.

She cycles home, and everything in Mom's past is making a noise. Dad is a fiend, an evil spirit. Down, down, down. It is like wading through quicksand.

But one evening something happens. One Saturday evening.

They are sitting at the kitchen table with a glass of wine, and Ninne and Ia are out. Mom is calm this evening, or so it seems, but suddenly she asks a question that leaves the girl dumbstruck. *Are you sleeping with him?* This unexpected question about her boyfriend drives her out into unfamiliar terrain; visibility is poor and there are menacing shadows.

Her throat contracts and she doesn't answer. At which point her mother places a hand on hers. *Do you enjoy it?* In that second something is severed. The question is greedy, voracious, intrusive. If she replies, whatever she says could be turned against her on another occasion. It has happened many times before.

Everything can be turned against her, and she never knows when that might be.

She is cut off. She is naked, like the child on the match-boxes. She staggers through bitter cold toward a gray planet, desolate and dead. It is difficult to describe the moment, almost impossible. They have grown together, they have been that way since the beginning of life, she and Mom. They are one single body made up of membranes, blood, and internal organs.

Being rejected by Mom is painful, but intimacy is even worse. Perhaps this is a rare moment when Mom actually sees her for once. And she just wants to get away. Anywhere. Far, far away. To any extinct planet whatsoever.

I have grown old, Mom goes on, turning her wineglass around and around. The days have gone whirling away out of the diary, a snowstorm of days. One day she woke up in an unfamiliar room, which is an old woman's body.

How is that possible? Mom wonders with undisguised amazement.

In silence she contemplates the unfamiliar room that is her mother's body; it has grown thin and scraggy. She is suddenly aware of her mother's sexual needs. She is seized by the idea that Mom wants to know what sleeping with her boyfriend is like because she is envious. A repulsive thought. It shuts her inside her mother's body. From that moment she knows that she has to get away from her.

But Mom refuses to be diverted.

You do know that a woman who sleeps with more than two men before she gets married is a *fallen woman*? Thank God, at last the paralysis is broken. She is furious, and rediscovers her voice. What crap.

Who's ever heard of a fallen man?

She refuses to give in, and she actually manages to make Mom laugh eventually. Deep inside she decides to become a fallen woman. She is going to sleep with twenty, fifty, a hundred. Or more. Men and women. She will be the author of her own *Decameron*, with herself as the courtesan and protagonist.

So I've finally made a decision about my future, she thinks ironically afterward.

However, strangely enough, when she sleeps with her boyfriend or with others in the future, she has to press her thighs together very tightly in order to prevent her mother's face from popping up between them. Like a pitch-black rose.

Unhappy. And reproachful. A black rose that blooms, withers, and dies. A perverse fantasy that I have never managed to find in the canon of psychology. This obsession, palpable and painful, pursued me for a long time, and forced me to think long and hard about mothers and daughters.

•   •   •

It turns out that Ricki has undergone many examinations, because her lightheadedness won't go away. Now she is in the hospital. She had an operation, it failed, they operated again. Dad is in Stockholm, and together they go to visit Olle on Drottninghusgränd.

He is putting the boy to bed when they arrive; it takes a while. He is thinner than ever; the furrow between his eyebrows, which meet in the middle, is deeper and makes him look stressed and hunted. It is a long evening, and a great deal of cognac is consumed. Olle's stomach ulcer has burst.

He has been forced to employ a nanny, she is very young, but it's her day off. Olle works long hours at Philips, and the hospital visits are the only bright spots in his day.

He misses Ricki every single second.

The boy is five years old, and on the whole he's doing fine. He never asks about Ricki, even though she's been away for quite a long time. He is talking at last, but in his own particular way. Comic book style. Olle imitates him: *Slam, bam. Danged kids! Watch out, run for your lives, crash, bam, help!*

And all in such a shrill, ear-splitting monotone that Olle is afraid the neighbors will hear and think he is abusing his son.

Both he and the nanny are exhausted. Don't get him wrong, he loves his precious boy, but the child is strong-willed, everything has to happen exactly the way he wants. Brushing his teeth must take two minutes; one second over and they have to start again. It as if the boy can make himself feel at home in the world only by imposing his will, his rules, and his meticulous but peculiar restrictions, Olle says.

Dad thinks the boy should be allowed to go and see Ricki.

Absolutely not, Olle replies. Not under any circumstances.

It would just mess things up. The boy might get yet more *idées fixes*. He might start insisting on visiting her every day, making life increasingly difficult for them. And even worse: Ricki might not recognize him.

Not recognize him — what the hell is wrong with her?

Olle doesn't answer the question, but he curses the doctors, fucking dilettantes, everything takes such an unconscionably long time, Ricki should have been home by now. Precious Mommy will get better, anything else is unthinkable. Ricki is the light of his life, his lucky star.

She wants to go and visit Ricki in the hospital. We'll see, Olle says. Outside it is getting darker. The glasses are refilled. Dad invites Olle and the boy to the house in the archipelago, he needs to rest. We'll see, Olle says again. In the middle of the night the precious boy appears in the doorway like a little white ghost.

Olle has to put him back to bed, once again it takes ages. Every time they make a move to leave, Olle begs them to stay. They are there for hours.

And Olle talks about himself: straight after his birth he was placed with a foster family. He has never met his biological mother, although he has tried to trace her. The only thing he has of her is a blurred photograph of a young girl with braids.

Not being recognized by his mother — that's something I don't want our son to experience, he says.

No, he doesn't want the boy to visit Ricki.

There are different kinds of loneliness. Olle's is mute. No access. Only Ricki has found her way in. When they finally leave, it has grown light outside. They walk across St. Johannes churchyard in the early dawn. The air is clear, not a cloud in the sky. It is quiet, there is no traffic yet.

Butterflies among the gravestones. And birds.

It will be fine, she says. Otherwise why would they have operated? You can never rule out the possibility of a miracle, Dad replies. By the steps leading down to Sveavägen she watches as he walks away.

She turns back and sits down on the grass in the churchyard. She wraps her arms around her knees and gazes out across the gravestones. In spite of the fact that she hasn't slept, she feels light and rested. A cat catches her eye.

Its tail is wagging slowly; it is on a journey of discovery. Then a girl comes along in grubby jeans; she raises a hand in greeting and asks for a cigarette. She sits down a short distance away, smoking. Her back is hunched, the nape of her neck white and fragile. Two lonely girls among all these dead people.

She unexpectedly sees herself from behind. Her neck is as thin as a six-year-old's. On the floor of the nursery with Ninne, who is wearing a red-checked dress. A ray of sunlight between the beds, Ninne refusing to put on her knee socks. Put on your seeknocks, Ninne! And Ninne rolls around laughing, wanting to hear *seeknocks* over and over again. Along with the other words they once shared.

Ia sleeps in the smallest room, which is no bigger than a closet. She has asked Mom if Ia can be her very own baby, and Mom has said yes.

Then she sees herself from behind in Granny's rock garden, with a dragonfly on her finger. Everyone in the house is fast asleep, only she and the dragonfly are awake. It breathes with the rear end of its body. And then it is gone.

In Årsta, as Ricki unrolls her architectural drawings.

In the schoolyard, wearing that loathsome beret. Herself from behind, from a long distance away, or is it backward? Staying in Lund means fossilizing. Better to opt for a broken heart and occasional clarity of vision and the freedom to breathe. It will mean carrying an enormous burden of guilt.

But fossilizing into a bad-tempered sack of stones would be much worse.

She comes back to the present, and the other girl has disappeared. She gets to her feet and leaves the churchyard. They catch the morning boat to the house in the archipelago, she and Dad. And they remain silent almost all the way, because what is there to say?

Olle comes over with the boy. Ninne and Ia are there too. Olle wants to talk to Dad on his own, so the sisters take their little cousin down to the shore for a swim. As they begin to get undressed, he starts howling like a wild animal; he runs up the hill and takes cover behind a pine tree.

They can see him peering around the trunk.

He is a very strange child.

He approaches them slowly. When they turn around: piercing yells, earsplitting screams, and he runs and hides behind a birch. They see his blond head moving from tree to tree, and they can't stop laughing at him. Until they realize it's the sight of their breasts the boy can't stand. They seem to remind him of something: a loss.

She pictures Ricki and the silent boy beneath her white breast: the image of the *Pietà*. They stop laughing and get dressed; the boy calms down. By now Olle is grateful that she wants to visit Ricki. He gives her a set of keys to the apartment.

But first of all she has to go and see Mom.

• • •

It is a farewell. Don't go, Mom keeps repeating quietly. It's only for a year, she replies, it's a lie, but it makes the situation more bearable. Gothenburg isn't all that far from Lund, I'll be back to see you all the time.

Don't go. Please, please don't leave me. Not you as well. You don't have to live at home, but stay in Lund.

Mom, I have to go.

Her mother falls silent, rubbing her fingers.

They are sitting on the balcony at her maternal grandparents' new two-room apartment in Gärdet. The market garden is to be sold; Mom has been helping them to pack everything up and is about to go back to Lund. Down below the balcony the birch leaves are rustling gently, and the terns are screaming in the sky. In Mom's eyes she sees the child with mixed blood who has always had to defend herself: enormous tension, enormous tenacity. But now abandoned. Utterly abandoned.

And she repeats that she has to get away, just for a while, gain some kind of perspective, have the chance to be herself. Her mouth is dry as she says it all again. Dead words. Like walking through a dead landscape, short steps, vigilance, silence.

Has her mother ever had the chance to be herself? Oh yes. Through her music. And in her language. Mom has been herself more than most people.

Eventually Mom gives up.

In that case I guess you have to go, she says.

In this life we live as if we were occupying a rented room. Language is also a room. Everything on loan. To be returned. We can't share death, but we can dig out a hollow and lie in it, settle down to wait: that's how it feels to say goodbye to Mom.

One step toward death. But one step closer to life.

Mom, I don't know if I can do it, but I'm going to try to write. She hasn't confided this to anyone else. And at that moment a little spark of interest is born in Mom's eyes.

Talking to Mom has gone better than she could have hoped. She goes with Mom to the central station, and on the platform they hug each other tightly.

She waves until the train is out of sight.

She unlocks the front door of the apartment on Drottninghusgränd. The place smells summer-empty. She opens the kitchen window, fries the blood pudding she has brought with her. Pinches a glass of cognac out of Olle's bottle.

What is she going to do with herself now she is all alone?

She is me. Or at least, I was once her.

I try to picture her in my mind's eye. She is wearing a turquoise summer dress and sandals. She doesn't know what to do. She crouches down in front of the bookcase in the dark hallway and reads the names on the spines.

She finds a book about Spinoza, but she doesn't have the energy to read.

The apartment is dark and depressing. Opening all the windows doesn't help; it is still stuffy. She pulls off her dress and drops it on a chair, walks around barefoot in her underwear.

She has made a big decision, and now she is scared. She is planning to move to a city she knows very little about.

Her boyfriend lives there. The relationship will end.

It mustn't end. But she doesn't love him, and it has to end.

She takes off her bra and panties and stands in the bathtub under the shower. She is crying, her tears mingled with the running water. She hasn't cried for a very long time. She hardly ever cries. And never uncontrollably, like this. It doesn't matter, it's okay to cry. No one can hear her. Her hair, which is usually caught up in a ponytail in a rubber band, is hanging loose; it is soon lank and sodden.

She sits on the edge of the bath and towels it dry. Calm.

She must calm down. There are things to do. She finds the linen cupboard and makes up the bed where she is to sleep, the boy's narrow bed with his Donald Duck comics in neat piles beside it. She gets into the bed. The ceiling is white and blind. She draws up her knees, the bead is swollen and hard. She masturbates. Enterprisingly, systematically.

For them, she thinks. The depressing apartment is the home of love. This is where she has met them. And only here. Her vagina, she pushes her finger deep inside, but it brings no relief.

The loneliness is too great. Loneliness is the song of the earth. *Das Lied von der Erde* by Gustav Mahler. Kathleen Ferrier. It washes over her, the grief: fierce and harsh. She fetches the bottle of cognac from the kitchen. She doesn't drink. She sits on the edge of the bed with her thighs spread apart and waters her pussy. Not waters. She rubs the golden, gleaming liquid over her labia with her finger.

Quietly. As a form of solace. Like a ritual. To calm herself.

She cannot calm herself. The grief overwhelms her, unmanageable and raging. Dad isn't coming back. They were a pentagram, it was blown apart and the pieces flew in all directions. She throws herself facedown on the bed.

Her shoulders are shaking, the tears pouring down her cheeks. She doesn't notice, but I can see her. It hurts. It hurts so much. She has held back for a long time. She misses us. And those five are gone, and will never exist again. They were not a pentagram.

How long does this go on?

Quite a long time, I think. I am the only one who can see her.

It goes on until she becomes aware of herself. Outside the August darkness has fallen. The pigeons are silent now; she closes the kitchen window and replaces the bottle of cognac in Olle's cupboard.

She contemplates her reflection in the bathroom mirror. Her face is swollen, and she doesn't recognize herself. The only time her grief was given free rein, and it was so tumultuous. A catharsis. She falls asleep at last.

•　•　•

In the morning she folds up the used sheets. She makes herself a coffee and rinses the cup under the faucet. Olle told her to catch the red bus; she gets off at Ringvägen.

She stands there looking up at the hospital.

Did it really remind her of a palace? Did I really scramble up through the undergrowth and the bushes in my sandals, unable to find the asphalt path? Am I remembering incorrectly, was it such a hot day? Everything was exactly like that.

It was an unusually hot August day.

She stops several times on her way to the hospital. Perhaps Ricki will be haggard and ugly. She doesn't want to remember her like that. The last meeting, if this is the last one, can obliterate all others. She sits down on the ground.

A bumblebee is buzzing in a clump of nettles nearby. She can see a plane up above, on its way to Bromma. The sky is blue and slightly curved, like a metal dish in a hot oven. She thinks about the prediction that promised Ricki two sons. Grandpa also believes in miracles, although he calls it the progress of medical science. Like Olle, he is convinced that Ricki will get better.

Maybe she won't recognize her.

That's possible.

But she will still be Ricki. People come and go through the main doors. An ambulance pulls up, a patient is wheeled in on a gurney. An old man is sitting on a bench by the wall, hunched over his stick. She sits down beside him and gropes in her pocket for a cigarette.

She smokes it, then stubs it out with her heel.

In the reception area she is directed to an elevator. She changes to a different elevator. An auxiliary is mopping the floor, and there is a smell of detergent. She follows a nurse along a corridor with lots of doors, some half-open. The nurse taps on Ricki's door. She is in a private room in a bed by the window, and doesn't notice that she has a visitor. The nurse touches her shoulder.

And Ricki turns her head and recognizes her. Immediately. With no hesitation whatsoever! Her face lights up; she is glowing.

Neta, how lovely, now we can have coffee!

I am telling the story as I remember it. Ricki was wearing a white hospital gown that barely met across her chest. She had put on a huge amount of weight. Otherwise she hadn't really changed, or so I thought at first.

Coffee with something to dip in it, she insisted.

It's not coffee time, the nurse objected.

Oh, come on, Ricki persisted. Coffee with something sweet, now my lovely niece has come to see me.

We're on a diet, the nurse warned. Ricki wasn't listening; she simply reeled off her list of requests. Danish pastries, cinnamon buns, cookies, sponge cakes. Anything sweet — crisprolls with jelly, if there's nothing else.

Surely you must have Danish?

You know perfectly well that you're on a diet, the nurse repeated as she left the room. I told Ricki that Olle sent his love, and her face lit up again: my darling husband! She was indescribably fat, shapeless, billowing, overflowing. Her hair had been hacked off just above shoulder level. But that wasn't what made her different; it was her brain.

She could recall things from long ago. Me. And Olle, of course. She hadn't a clue that she had given birth to a much longed-for son.

Ricki no longer remembered her five-year-old!

She lay in sunlight, but she was on her way into the shadows. Her room was at the top of the main building of the Southern District Hospital, almost touching the sky, and overlooking Årstaviken. Way down below the water sparkled and the sailboats sped along. Ricki rested in the sunlight as if it were a cradle. The visit was more important for me than for her; she would soon forget it.

She hasn't changed, I tried to convince myself.

The kindness, that bright clarity, the optimism.

The essential nature of her personality, I tried to tell myself.

But that wasn't quite true. I would never be able to ask her about the things I had wanted to discuss. Love. Dad. And Mom. Or Spinoza — I knew a little more about him by that stage.

I pulled a chair close to the bed. Ricki was interested only in Danish pastries. She kept anxiously asking about them. After about an hour an auxiliary actually appeared with a tray of coffee, pastries, and cookies, balancing it adeptly on Ricki's enormous belly.

Ricki devoted her full attention to the goodies and ate up every scrap, until only crumbs remained. She sighed and licked her fingers so that she could finish every last one.

Delicious, she said, beaming from ear to ear. Absolutely delicious.

By the time she had finished polishing the plate, she was feeling sleepy. I hugged that big body and left. I trudged along the endless corridors, went down in one elevator after another, and left the hospital via the main entrance.

I went and sat on a rock up above Årstaviken. The air was still warm. Across the water I thought I could just make out the apartment block on Sijansvägen.

The white sails of the yachts billowed in the wind.

A green subway train passed over the railway bridge heading south, as silent as an illusion, high above the running water. Ricki would die by running water, according to an unknown fortune-teller at the beginning of time.

It suddenly seemed to me that I could see many dead people hovering above the water: their eager faces, their insistent voices, their strange lives.

Is it possible to hang out with the dead? Talk to them?

Yes. Maybe it's better with them.

What was most important, the tumor or the love? I was filled with conviction: the love. It passes through those of us who are alive; it is then gathered in something greater and returns. What that is we will never know, but one of the many names of that unknown quantity is solace.

That was what our meeting was like; it was the last time I saw Ricki.

Then I stood on Ringvägen waiting for the bus. I was on my way to the future. It was very uncertain. The bus would take me there.

The last of the afternoon sunlight reached me. Before it disappeared the red bus arrived, and I got on. It rattled across Västerbron. Dad had driven Mom and me home across that bridge when my existence had only just begun. I knew that I loved them.

That I had to leave them.

The bus continued along by the water. People were walking on the shore in the dying summer light. Babies in strollers. Dogs. Everything was as it was, and nothing could be changed. I had been locked inside a prison. Not entirely, but to a certain extent, I had built it myself. Therefore, I was also able to leave it.

I was filled with gratitude, toward Ricki most of all. She was going to die, but she had opened her life to joy. And everything was opening up around me, the city and the people. Life is born precisely where the darkness meets the light, and I think we can call that God.

I would collect every little seed of joy in my hands.

I think it was something along those lines that went through my mind on the red bus.

And it was a revelation. An epiphany. I have had to use many words to find my way to this memory. The sun was gone, but the light remained for a long time, over the waters of the city and within me.

The quotations at the beginning of the four sections
are taken from Marguerite Duras, *Écrire* (1993),
translated into Swedish by Kennet Klemets (2014).

Stockholm and Yxlan
2013–2015

AGNETA PLEIJEL was born in Stockholm in 1940. One of Sweden's foremost novelists, she is also a playwright and poet. Her books have been translated into more than twenty languages. She has worked as a critic and cultural editor for various Swedish newspapers and magazines. Pleijel served as president of the Swedish chapter of PEN International between 1987 and 1990, and has been a member of the academy Samfundet de Nio (the Nine Society) since 1988. From 1992 to 1996 she was a professor at the Institute of Drama in Stockholm.

MARLAINE DELARGY has translated novels by John Ajvide Lindqvist, Kristina Ohlsson, and Helene Tursten, as well as *The Unit* by Ninni Holmqvist and Therese Bohman's *Drowned* and *The Other Woman*. She lives in England.

KATHERINE CARLYLE by Rupert Thomson

Unmoored by her mother's death, Katherine Carlyle abandons the set course of her life and starts out on a mysterious journey to the ends of the world.

"The strongest and most original novel I have read in a very long time... It's a masterpiece."
—Philip Pullman, author of the best-selling His Dark Materials trilogy

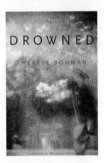

DROWNED by Therese Bohman

This spellbinding novel of psychological suspense combines hothouse sensuality with ice-cold fear on every page.

"Bohman could be lumped in with the other Scandinavian authors since *The Girl with the Dragon Tattoo*, but her story is more quiet and nuanced, her writing lush enough to create a landscape painting with every scene." —*O, The Oprah Magazine*

QUICKSAND by Malin Persson Giolito

An incisive courtroom thriller and a drama that raises questions about the nature of love, the disastrous side effects of guilt, and the function of justice

"Giolito's astonishing English-language debut is a dark exploration of the crumbling European social order and the psyche of rich Swedish teens... Masterful." —*Booklist* (starred review)

"Powerful...A splendid work of fiction."
—*Kirkus Reviews*

Also recommended:

THE UNIT by Ninni Holmqvist

Named one of the Best Novels of the Year by the
Wall Street Journal, a gripping story about a society
in the throes of a cynical, utilitarian way of thinking
disguised as care

"Echoing work by Marge Piercy and Margaret
Atwood, *The Unit* is as thought-provoking as it is
compulsively readable." —Jessa Crispin, NPR.org

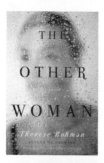

THE OTHER WOMAN by Therese Bohman

A psychological novel where questions of class,
status, and ambition loom over a young woman's
passionate love affair

"Bohman's characters are curiously, alarmingly awake,
and a story we should all know well is transformed
into something wondrous and strange. A disturbing,
unforgettable book." —Rufi Thorpe, author of
The Girls from Corona del Mar

WILLFUL DISREGARD by Lena Andersson

Winner of the August Prize, a novel about a perfectly
reasonable woman's descent into the delusions of
unrequited love

"Gripped me like an airport read...perfect."
—Lena Dunham

"*Willful Disregard* is a story of the heart written
with bracing intellectual rigor. It is a stunner,
pure and simple." —Alice Sebold, best-selling
author of *The Lovely Bones* and *Lucky*